Thank Your **Lucky Stars**

Thank Your Lucky Stars

short stories

Sherrie Flick

AUTUMN
HOUSE PRESS
Pittsburgh

pennsylvania
COUNCIL ON THE ARTS

Autumn House Press receives state arts funding support through a grant from the Pennsylvania Council on the Arts, a state agency funded by the Commonwealth of Pennsylvania, and the National Endowment for the Arts, a federal agency.

ISBN: 978-1-938769-35-1
Library of Congress Control Number: 2018941413

For **RICK**
and for **PAM**

I

How I Left Ned

I knew from the start the men who sold me the corn were not farmers. They didn't have the right look—the right peaceful demeanor. They did not *look* like farmers. Their clothes for instance and their hair. Now, their location was okay: Dirt road. Fields. Big blue sky. They had a pickup. But gold chains and razor stubble, perms. Soft, curly perms like poodles. Big black poodles dressed like Italian men, selling corn. Cologne. Hell, I'm no fool. A real farmer would shave before he struck out to sell some produce. Especially corn. Especially in Nebraska. And I believe farmers in general—with the public at least—are kind and gentle and generous. This has been my experience. These guys were going for pure profit. And there I was with my car idling, just expecting fairness.

I said I wanted four. Four ears, just so there was no confusion.

One of them said, "I'll sell you six for two dollars."

Now, I know as well as the next person that two dollars is

too high a price for anything less than a dozen of anything grown. I said, "Four."

He said, "I'll throw in an extra, make it seven."

I said, "Four."

He looked at me, smiled and shrugged. He said, "We only deal in bulk." He turned his back. The other one looked way off into the sky beyond my head as if he just expected me to float away and eventually make it into his line of vision.

By now I'm wanting the corn. *Wanting* it. I can see the sample ear. It looks fresh and young and perky. The way a young farmer would look waiting at church on Sunday to shake the preacher's wife's hand. Young. Perky. I wanted it. I did not, however, want these faux farmers messing with me. Ripping me off. Right in the middle of the Midwest.

I said, "Six. Okay. I'll make some friends, have a cookout. It'll be good for me to expand my social circle beyond me and Ned and the cat." These two fake farmers looked at each other like they had a secret, and then one picked up a bag and put eight ears in.

"Bulk," he said. He said it like he was saying, "Pussy." Like it was a threat.

I said, "Three dozen." Just to show him a thing or two. I folded my arms across my chest.

The other one who before this had been staring at my chest, raised his eyebrows real nonchalantly, like three dozen was like two, like it was nothing really, three dozen ears.

I said, "That would be thirty-six ears. A whole lot of corn." He looked at me like he had a whole crop of corn back at his farm— corn beside cows and a silo and some pigs. But I knew. No way. He lived in a seedy tenement building. He knew what a cockroach

2

looked like. I bet he couldn't even start a lawn mower let alone a John Deere to save his life. I knew. The corn was hot.

The guy with the bag said, "Three dozen. Why not make it four? Why stop at thirty-six when you could have forty-eight? Why not make a whole lot of friends while you're at this socializing?" I knew he was implying that I couldn't socialize if somebody paid me. I was getting pissed.

He was putting ears of corn in willy-nilly now, like he'd never stop. The bag was full up. A big grocery bag of corn there in the late afternoon sun. A big bag sitting on the gate of the faded red pickup. The sun shifted. The wind blew. And suddenly, like a brick in the head, I understood bulk food. The beauty of a silo of wheat. The immensity of thirty pounds of soy beans. The numbers. The quantity. The bulk.

I thought about Ned, about his organic lentils and his rice cakes. About his fat content and antioxidant obsession, about his juicer. I thought about Ned spooning exactly one level teaspoon of nonfat sour cream onto his microwaved baked potato every Wednesday night as a special treat. I thought about Ned tying his condom into a little knot when he was done, pulling a Kleenex from the box beside the bed—dabbing himself and pecking me on the cheek.

I thought then about pounds of butter, gallons of whole milk—ears of corn. I thought about ears and ears and ears. Then I thought about divorce.

The fake farmer still reclining in the lawn chair, the one without the bag, the one with the Catholic-looking medallion sitting on his hairy exposed chest, had lit up a cigarette. He inhaled slowly, squinting his eyes. He looked at me and said, "Hell, hon. We'll give you a deal on this whole truckload if you want. Think about the possibilities."

He smiled like he was making a joke. Then he was laughing like the joke he was making was funny.

I said, "You know. Confidentially. Ned is an asshole."

The two fake farmers looked at each other with sly grins. "This Ned," one said with a wink, "we could take care of him, you know. Teach him to appreciate corn, if necessary."

Crickets made noises all around. Cars zoomed from up on the interstate. I heard the whirring of big bugs off in the distance— the kind I really don't like to think about.

I knew they had found some farmer somewhere, stole his truck, his corn, probably shot his dog.

I smiled. I said softly, "Did anyone see?"

One thrust the full sack toward me. The other stood up and coughed, smoothed the crease running along the front of his pants.

"We better be going," he said.

I said, "Okay." I headed toward the passenger door of their truck.

He said, "No *we* better be going. We've got some corn to eat. Things to do."

I smiled. I said, "I *like* corn. I like to eat it. I like to look at it. I like to sell it." I looked one, then the other, straight in the eye. Slowly, I said, "I don't mind quality produce one bit."

And this was the way we came to an understanding.

I left my car right there, engine running. I hopped in, holding on to my bulging bag.

Down the road a few miles the one behind the wheel said, "Just to be fair. That'll be five-fifty."

After I handed over the money, he said, "Much obliged."

It was then I noticed his Italian loafers. I put my hand on

one fake farmer knee, then another. I looked straight ahead. I asked about dinner, about the possibilities of building a small stand where we could settle down for a while. They both nodded. I turned up the country music on the radio. I thanked my lucky stars.

Crickets

C rickets come out at night in small country towns. They sing like pleasant car alarms again and again. Again and again. In their little black jumpsuits, they take to the crooked sidewalks in droves, not hesitating to leave the flowers and grasses. They come to the sidewalks, and they hop. They hop with all their might. They spring and jump in the bright streetlight stadium like fireworks. And when a person comes strolling along, the crickets call that fate.

Dance

Vivian sips her whiskey in the den where her thoughts waver between doom and joy. In her mind, Viv has always had a tumbler of whiskey in one hand. Her other hand waves around in conversation like a tiny bird. That hand used to habitually hold a cigarette, but not anymore.

Vivian is slumped into the leather chair, worn in the right places. She's half in shadow, half light. After she retired from her teaching job, all of that schoolbook knowledge settled inside her like a sand dune. Ideas and concepts flit through her thoughts, shimmer and dull. She picks up her book. Sets it down.

Vivian whispers and her voice cracks as it carries down the hallway asking Matty to get her more ice for her drink. He always hears her, eventually. By the time he shows up, cubes dripping through his clawed fingers, Viv is repeating, "ice, ice, ice," letting the *sssss* slide through her front teeth like a piece of stretched ribbon.

Matty plunks the sweating cubes into the glass. *Ploink, ploink, ploink. Ploink.*

"Always with this drama, Viv. Really," he says. "You could walk down the hallway yourself and get the damn ice." Then, glancing at the wall beyond the windows, he says, "You know, y'all shouldn't be day drinking like losers in here. At least try the patio. Jesus." Matty brushes away a few crumbs from his apron. Viv watches as they fall like little shooting stars to the floor between them. His apron is lime green with white flowers festooned down its front, a ruffle along the neckline. It once belonged to Viv. Now that Matty has sold his construction company the apron's ties wrap his thick middle with a bow.

"There's just one of me, Matty. Who, may I ask, are you talking about with 'y'all'?" Vivian flits her hand, follows the expanse of the den wall—its sports trophies, hardbound books, and taxidermied deer head.

Matty nods at the deer. "I'm including Mr. Bojangles in my musings. Those eyes beg for some inclusion. At minimum." He pats the deer's nose, which looks convincingly wet and alive. The deer head is from a different time in their lives. It has an air of archaeological remains and helps assure Matty that it wasn't always like this.

After Matty retreats to the kitchen, Viv lifts the deer head from its screw, leaving a ghost shadow on the rosy wallpaper. She carts it to the patio with her drink. She likes how it weighs down her free arm. She's surprised at its heft as she shuffles out into the clear light.

Mr. Bojangles looks both unhappy and unimpressed when she props him up in the metal chair. A dragonfly explores the space above his ears, then flits away.

"I don't give one flying fuck," she tells the deer. Viv sits up straighter to accommodate this sentiment. The deer winks at her. But Viv won't give into that kind of flirtation. She reaches to pet its nose like Matty did, but reconsiders. "Your eyelashes are fake," she tells the deer. "They are fake," she assures herself, blinking. She wants to pour the deer a drink. Instead, she has a good stare down with him. She's sure Mr. Bojangles is judging her. "Fucker," she says. She taps her fingers on the edge of the patio table, her nails making the tiniest drumroll on the thin metal. "I know what you need," she says, and Viv shifts the deer so it's sitting in profile, waiting for its deer friends to arrive. "Better?" she asks, then settles into her own patio chair and her own thoughts, wandering from Proust to Previn to Picasso.

"It is more decent on the patio, don't you agree?" she asks the deer after a time. The air is clear, and the waxy sound of crickets mixes with light traffic noises. The pretty potted plants Matty has tended to, over-tended to really, sit silently sober like overdressed introverts come to the wrong party. Vivian gives them a long look, wraps one leg over another, and squints at the view. A wooden fence and a brick wall are all she can see, and she can hear some neighborhood children, girls, squealing with delight in the distance, playing some kind of game. Tag? Bloody Murder? She can't tell.

Viv shakes her head, which clears it a little. She flips her unruly hair behind her shoulders. Her hair was once a vibrant, head-turning copper. Viv was a stunner. She knows this. "I used to turn heads, Mr. Bojangles," she whispers. She pats at her curls. "What brings you to this little outpost, anyway?" she asks, reaching her free hand across the table, tapping a finger to get the deer's attention.

Viv's pantsuit is terry cloth. The sunny yellow with its white piping gave her a blip of cheer this morning when she pulled it on over her skinny thighs. Her bony hands are loaded down with ruby rings, one on each finger. Her birthday, July. Ruby, her stone. Blood, blood red, she thinks. "Don't even," she says to the deer. She removes the rings, setting them on the table like a wager. She wishes she had a deck of cards.

It's late August. Viv sips at her whiskey. She sucks at an ice cube. She jiggles the glass. "It's watered down now," she confesses to the deer. She knows early evening is coming because the state of her tumbler is a clock she reads like a sundial.

Inside, Matty looks out the window at Viv. She's leaning toward the deer like they're conspiring. The light from the nearby apple tree dapples the table and chairs like a school of fish.

Matty knows he's been more productive since the incident. "Meeting goals," he tells the dough he's kneading. He rocks it firm and steady for tomorrow's bread. "It's been years now," he tells the kitchen. The dough transforms from sticky to elastic under his thrusting, floured palms. Viv drinking and reading while he bakes and cooks is a good solution for them these days. He kneads the dough, rolls crusts, slices apples, peaches, and pears. He bakes and bakes and the minutes pass like magic tricks he's seen a thousand times but never ceases to be amazed at. A fine puff of flour rises up when he swats his belly.

Matty sips at the cooking sherry. No one is watching. He nestles the bread dough into a bowl for a slow rise. He *plop-plops* some of the sherry into the sliced pears a group of neighborhood girls dropped off yesterday. He fingers in some nutmeg. He works the pears toward his pie. Translucent slices, the sugar dissolving, daring that crust to come closer. Most likely the girls from the neighborhood stole the pears from a neighbor's tree while that person was at work. The girls can be sneaky and conniving, especially when they get roaming in a pack like that. They steal berries from the alleyways, tomatoes from gardens, and sometimes a bottle of gin from a stash in someone's cellar.

It's a close neighborhood on St. Anthony Street. Viv and Matty have lived here a long time now. Matty's family used to go way down around this block and up the next. His mom used to bake treats for everyone, but she's gone. They're all gone now. Still, the neighbors talk—not too much, and never to him about anything that matters. Never about the incident. These days Matty feels just fine. That's the truth. He feels like he has been and always will be fine.

The girls come and go up the front porch steps, dropping off what they're given to deliver: apples, concord grapes, fresh mint. Their mothers make them do it, and then they make the girls go back with dollars folded into the soft spaces of their tiny front pockets to buy the pastries Matty bakes. He takes orders every Monday. He's tacked up a chalkboard on the far wall to keep track of everything. He lists his regulars, lists his fruits and nuts, lists what he plans to bake. The girls run off to tell their moms and the moms call their orders in to Matty. They talk quickly and quietly on the phone as if they don't want their husbands to hear, as if they're telling him a secret. Sometimes they ask him for something special, like these hand pies. Matty always says yes.

Every Friday, he wipes the board clean and starts over again.

Matty crimps the soft top crust to the bottom, pinching the dough into a zigzag around the pan. He has carved a few delicate flowers on the top crust as steam vents for the baking pie. The flowers are in the shape of the idea of daisies. It's a bundled up nest of lush sweetness when he's finished sealing it.

He brushes some milky water over the top, slides it into the oven. The oven's heat slaps at Matty's face, scorches his arms. He clicks on the timer, then gently stacks the sugary hand pies he finished earlier in the day into a paper sack. He eats one. Can't help himself. Raspberries, brown sugar, and walnuts with a tiny bit of mascarpone. He's gaining weight, he knows.

The breeze shimmies the treetops outside the kitchen window. The leaves flip and flop in the late-day sun. A gorgeous day, and Matty finds himself dancing across the linoleum floor. He hums to the shaking trees' rhythm, twisting his bulging hips and sliding a slippered foot. He pumps his arms, smooths the kitchen air with his hands. As he pivots near the dishwasher he remembers those dark nights at the bar with Viv, disco dancing until two. They owned the place. That red hair of hers, always a beacon, bringing him to shore. They'd hug their hips to the bar afterward. Ordering another final, final round. Bonfires at the ocean on weekends, out beyond the dunes and the rutted lane. Big smiles with white teeth exposed, heads thrown back. Laughing, the tide rolling in. And then in the fire's shadow he's not sitting with Viv anymore. She's not sitting with him. The whole world had a different sheen back then. It was all Technicolor and denim. Driving with Jane, with Dee-Dee, no regrets, windows down like in a movie. The sun blip-blipping their soundtrack. Salty air. Seagulls. That sour taste of Sarah's too-young skin luring him in. Keeping him for a time when it didn't seem wrong. Nothing did. And then that night on Fishbone Street. Fishtailing and the silence that comes before impact. The bright, soundless ring of before. But that's over now. Behind him. Behind them.

Outside his kitchen right now he hears the sound of screeching tires. No thud for impact, just indistinguishable voices and some yelling. Just another close call.

Lulu Smith, a neighbor's girl, trots up the steps, her hair a blonde mane secured high on her head with a thick elastic. She catches him dancing alone and Matty is embarrassed. He flattens his hand over his aproned belly, adjusts the collar on his shirt. He taps on the radio news, as he says, "Well, howdy-do, Princess Blue?" The stern, practiced NPR voice makes everything around him dull down to a crisp gray.

Lulu adjusts her ponytail, looks quickly toward the screen door she has just come through. She radiates summer, swimming, healthy snacks. Her Adidas sparkle, her creamy white ankle socks sit just so. Her athletic shorts are snug like she will never have a care in the world. Matty remembers that she might be on the tennis team. Or she likes horses. He can't remember which.

Lulu pops her gum. She does not pretend that she didn't see Matty dancing his way across the floor. "Hello Mr. Matty," she says. "Mama says hello. She says to say hello to Mrs. Viv, too." Lulu pushes one foot slightly forward, probably a remnant position from ballet class. She has brought some rhubarb, big long sticks of it from her mother's garden, wedged into a plastic shopping bag. "Mom says to give you this." Lulu tilts her head, holds the bag like a bouquet of roses in her skinny arms.

Matty takes the rhubarb from Lulu, gets a whiff of its stringent sour pie potential as he shifts the bag to the counter. He imagines the cup of sugar he'll pour over top once it's rinsed clean and chip-chopped into a bowl. He knows the rhubarb bits will greedily suck the sugar in. He looks at Lulu, who is waiting for him to say something. Her porcelain skin catches the light, and Matty feels a longing, a now unfamiliar longing, that leaves him speechless for a moment. He's transported back in time and then instantly back to this moment here.

"Well," he finally says. "Here's those hand pies your mama special ordered." Matty brushes Lulu's fingers as he gives her the crisp bag of goodies. Their hands touch when he takes the moist bills from her. "If you see SallyAnn, tell her that her mama's pear pie will be ready tomorrow morning." Lulu takes note with a quick nod that sways her ponytail, and she's gone.

"Bye, Lulu," he says too quietly because she has already trotted down the stairs back into her summer day.

Matty washes his hands. He wipes them carefully dry. He changes into a clean apron. He doesn't usually change into a new apron this soon and wonders why he's doing it now, but it feels nice—crisp and clean. This one sports a giant parrot down the front with a violent blue background. Who knows where it came from. He looks out to Viv again.

"And?" she yells from the patio.

"And what?" Matty yells back, pulling the long red sticks of rhubarb from the shopping bag that reads, THANK YOU. HAVE A NICE DAY! in scrolling yellow cursive. The rhubarb is crusted with a layer of fine sandy dirt. He wants to wash it clean right away. Wants to get it going.

"How's the pastry chef?" Viv says.

"It was fine. I'm fine," Matty calls back, his voice cracking. "Lulu. Jenny's girl. She picked up those hand pies, dropped off rhubarb. She reminds me of a horse the way she trots around."

Viv grunts to acknowledge the observation. "Mr. Bojangles

needs a drink," she shout-talks. "I'm drinking with a deer," she says.

Matty nods in Viv's general direction, happy Mr. Bojangles has been brought into play on the patio. He considers making the deer a drink. A nice dry martini. Gin. Or a gimlet. He cuts a piece of rhubarb from the stalk, runs it under cold water, then sticks the stalk's end into the sugar bowl. He bites down and chews. The quick rush of sweet-and-sour in his mouth is exactly what he needs. He considers making himself a martini, but decides he will drink a little more sherry. Maybe later on he'll have one, staring up at the full moon from the patio with Viv.

Matty measures flour, rubs in butter, preps scones for the morning. He zests a lemon, rubs its sharp sunshine into the sugar before adding it to the bowl.

Matty contemplates dinner. Sliced tomatoes with some bleu cheese in a quiche crust. Fat, eggs, cheese, salt. The oven chugs along. He can't wait to smell that quiche baking. He'll add a side salad and make a fresh raspberry vinaigrette. As Viv shrinks to nothing he fattens himself up. He imagines flying up and out of this neighborhood like a big, fat hot-air balloon. He's already far away when Viv comes tottering down the hallway toward the kitchen. Her uneven slipper heels tip-tap on the wooden floor. She clears her throat, sets her tumbler down gently, carefully, in the sink.

Both hands free, she can't think of what to do or say next. She feels sad and vulnerable, naked in her own kitchen. Matty looks at her strangely, so she gives him a slow squeeze, a hug. She pulls Matty into her, feeling for his former body—the body she once knew—now buried under the pudge of Matty. She pushes into him, but he's not there. His middle gives way softly and then expands back. She steps away from the embrace, giving him a poke.

She remembers the day they bought Mr. Bojangles at the junk shop on Miller's Lane. The dust glittering in the dull light as they opened and closed the creaking front door of the store. The shelves overstuffed. She felt like she was saving the deer head, bringing it into a better home, a more interesting life, as she pulled it down from a hook on the wall. She hugged his wide furry neck in the front seat as they drove home past fields of fireflies.

She asks Matty if he remembers that day. The song "Mr. Bojangles" playing on the radio, and they named the deer like it was a pet. Then they hung him on the den wall, and their life went on in its crazy way until there was a little too much crazy, until the night he let Sarah drive. Sarah of the palest, finest porcelain skin. Sarah of the best drugs. Sarah laughing, driving the truck. Viv in the back seat making time with who knows who. It didn't matter who was who. She and Matty were unstoppable. Matty made the biggest mistake with Sarah, and then their lives came to a halt when the truck plowed into an oak tree. Though they have always survived, Sarah smashed through and out. Sarah's smashing a continuum, out and through, playing every so often like a silent movie.

"You bet I do," says Matty sadly, and it takes Viv a moment to realize what he's responding to. "How could I forget?"

Now Viv hums the song softly to herself while Matty turns back to his world, the kitchen counter, cracking six eggs into a bowl, whisking them fast and fluffy with a clop-clop noise. Did they just hug? Doesn't matter. Matty has returned to his task at hand: quiche. His back straight, his shoulders stiff.

Viv pours herself a drink. "And one for my furry friend," she says. She returns to the patio, fresh drinks, bright clinking cubes. One in each hand. She shuffles down the hallway. She slinks; she slithers; she moves down the hall like a winter draft. She smells salt air, bears witness to the deepening shadows that announce evening. A whiff of pear pie following close behind.

Sweetie Pie

I started calling both my dog and husband Sweetie Pie the same year my husband found my lover's cashmere sock. I'd stuffed it in my coat pocket after tugging at it slithered like a snake down my pant leg. But it escaped flaccidly onto our stone entryway. After walking my dog up and around the hill, the city nestled below us, its rivers aquiver, I unhooked the leash. I said, "Oh, Sweetie Pie. I'll always love you." Then, as the dog skittered to his kibble, I saw my husband's hand clutching the fine knit. I said, "Oh, Sweetie Pie."

Lenny the Suit Man

L enny scampers upstairs to our offices about once or twice a month. His van idles in the back parking lot: The Suit Van. With his tape measure, he crawls all over us at our desks. Phones ring. I'm trying to photocopy.

Gary says, "Lenny. Come off it. We got suits, see? We don't need anymore."

But Lenny has this way with people. He doesn't give up. His suits are nice and cheap. I'm moping in the corner, telling myself I'm not thinking about Valerie, even though I'm scratching V, V, V, along the border of my desktop planner.

I go down with the other guys. Lenny flicks his tape measure, trots ahead of us even though he knows our measurements by heart. That's why we like him—he's efficient, does his job, treats us right.

The suits aren't hot; he swears it, and you've got to believe him. There's something about his face. It tells you, hey, I've known pain. I don't need to steal suits.

That's what it tells me, anyway. I'm Bob, and I believe in Lenny.

Lenny chatters about fabric colors matching flecks in eyes and about quality—how it doesn't come knocking on your door every day. That's a joke. Lenny pauses, and when we laugh, he laughs too—a big chuckle for such a little man—which makes us laugh more. Lenny makes us happy even when the guys from upstate are making us crunch numbers, looking to satisfy another budget cut.

In his van, there's an espresso machine bolted to a piece of wood. He sets it on the driver's seat after parking. It runs off the cigarette lighter. I ask him why he doesn't get a regular coffee maker, tell him it would at least squirt out a decent amount. We stand around looking at suits, sipping espresso out of too-big white Styrofoam cups. Lenny insists, tells us it's classy and European, tells us we need class in order for his suits to reach their full potential. He apologizes for the cups, says he wants china, but his cousin Sandy got a deal on five cases of twelve-ounce Styrofoam. Lenny says Sandy says no china until the cups are gone. Sandy's an investor, so whatever he says goes.

I order a brown suit. I need it. Lenny says he'll bring it back in a couple of weeks, ready to fit my body like a glove should fit a hand.

The air is cool and crisp. The sky, bright blue. Everything anticipates winter. I'm not ready for winter or anything that's frozen and unstoppable. Yesterday, when it was raining like hell, I was the weather. Me. Right there. I didn't even use my umbrella—walked the whole way home in my dark blue single-breasted with nobody looking twice. Now the cold I don't deserve has started in. The brown suit is mine.

I haven't told Lenny about my smashed-up heart or let on about how Valerie yanked it out and tossed it down two flights of stairs. But he knows something's wrong. I should be jabbing him more about his coffee instead of just sitting here in his swiveled passenger seat, sipping it quietly, like some European guy who drinks this stuff every day with his ankles crossed, pinkie raised. The van is bigger than it looks from the outside. We can fit two, three guys inside easy, while the others mill about in the parking lot talking suits and sports scores.

I would like to mention pity. Pity. I hate it. It's those moist puppy-dog eyes people throw at you like they have any idea what you're going through. Like they know what Valerie said as she slammed the door and headed down the two flights of stairs from my apartment. Stomping, mind you, on my squishy, throbbing heart with each step—two harder stomps on the landing between the floors.

She said, "Bob. I don't date stupid guys."

I spent the last two nights listening to old country music. It's what I do under duress. The Patsy Cline cassette tape has started to stretch with all the repeated playing and threw a high-pitched whine this morning while I was in the shower. After work, I'm buying a new one.

Lenny sees right through it all—pulls me aside and says, "Fuck her. I can see that so-sad look on you, Bob. Don't let her get the best of you. Your measurements will change. I've seen it a million times."

I nod in Lenny's direction, swallowing hard. This whole interaction closes in on ominous. Goose bumps dot my arms; tears brim in public. I can't believe it. As Lenny hugs me, all my coworkers turn in unison to watch. This is the beginning of my problems. They end with Susan, but that's another story completely. I know my life is going to collapse before it puffs up. I'm certain my heart will never fit right again.

I ask to try on another suit and say, "Lenny. I'm not a stupid guy."

Lenny says, "No, Bob. No way," like he's trying to drive a point home—he looks at me like we have an inside joke about this. Lenny does not pity me or pat me on the shoulder, which is why I don't appreciate it when Gary walks up and does just that.

Three or four pats and Gary says, "You okay, Bob? Got what you want?"

In retrospect, I realize, I take this all wrong. Pity, I think. I hate it. I think, hell no. I am not okay. I did not want Valerie stomping down my stairs wearing my favorite flannel shirt I'd loaned her because she was cold.

So I whisper, "Gary, just fuck off."

This doesn't go over well. Gary is my boss and soon, without much wind-up, he's like I've never seen him. He's jogging back and forth with his fists curled and shoulders hunched. The van rocks, and he throws punches in my direction. He sputters something like, "Yeah, come at me. Yeah, come at me." Espresso spills onto the white linen double-breasted Stan just ordered for his spring vacation. I'm ducking and swallowing hard with my own fists feebly clenched in front of my face the way Father Vincent showed me the afternoon after Timmy Price smeared me across the Sacred Heart playground. I can taste the brine in my throat. Lenny remains calm. He's the only one who stays in the van as my coworkers rush out onto the sidewalk like lemmings.

Lenny says, "Gary. Gary." Real steady, like he's done it a million times. Suit jackets fly as Gary's in full force. Lenny methodically taps Gary on the forehead—somehow finding his forehead amongst the flurry of punches he's throwing mostly to the air. The tapping makes a soft thudding noise.

Gary slows as his fists make larger and larger windmills; his legs stop dancing, and he collapses onto the orange shag carpet of the van mumbling, "Lint." He rubs his face back and forth across the worn scratchy stubble.

I run out of the van, past my huddled and whispering coworkers, and across the parking lot toward the shrubbery by the marquee—bent over and on the verge of dry heaves. After a while, I pull a handkerchief carefully out of my back pocket and blow my nose. I grab the Tic Tacs out of my breast pocket.

Back in the van, Gary slowly stands up and Lenny steps out to mumble things at my coworkers who seem—from my limited point of view—more interested in my potential heaves than the thousands of punches their boss just threw. Gary didn't hit me once. He flogged a lot of hanging suits and, as I mentioned, the air, but he never touched me.

Lenny walks across the asphalt lot, puts his hands in his pockets, looking optimistic. He says, "Gary wouldn't hurt you, Bob. He's just under a lot of pressure these days. Downsizing. You understand. The brown suit's on me when it comes in. Totally free of charge."

Gary slinks over with apologies, talking softly about deadlines and a sick German shepherd at home. I nod my head, shuffle my feet, shrug, saying, "No harm done." Gary walks back into our building. Later he'll take me out for a beer.

Lenny looks off into the distance beyond his idling van toward the flat horizon and the plaza malls, antsy to get going. I say, "Hey man, thanks for doing that forehead thing. You probably saved my life."

Lenny shrugs, says, "Tai chi." I shake his hand. I don't like hugging guys.

The next month I'm at a party I don't want to be at, but my coworkers had started in on calling me a hermit. I pour myself a nice drink: short glass, ice, vodka. No fruit. Most people hate this, but I think it looks clean. Nothing like a nice clean drink. I'm sipping my vodka, looking over Joe's shoulder while he's beating Gary at cribbage. He's kicking Gary's ass, and I'm enjoying myself immensely because nobody feels the need to talk to me or check on me or anything. Joe really wants a promotion, but I know he's not getting one, so I'm happy he's at least getting some satisfaction. And then, wham. There she is: Valerie. She's at the one party I decide to attend in the four weeks since she ruined me. Valerie looks across the room, squints at me, and waves "hi" like I'm not a stupid guy at all, but a casual acquaintance whose name she just can't place right now but knows she should be polite to. She smiles. Someone takes her coat, which means she's staying.

I'm not even nervous that I'm about to have a breakdown standing on Bill and Tanya's pristine worsted wool carpet. They're very nice people in a seemingly healthy relationship, and they served shrimp cocktail specifically because it's my favorite. I wave back politely. I notice—and I may be wrong—the whole room stop, take a collective sigh, then kick in with their idle chatter again.

I think, yes, I see. Valerie and I are now the kind of people who wave across rooms.

Valerie is pleased with this transaction and nods like she would to an obedient dog. She heads toward the kitchen or maybe the bathroom. I don't know because I beeline it to the back door, sit on the steps smoking the pack of cigarettes I palmed from the coffee table on my way out. They're British or French or Canadian, shorter than American cigarettes, and tasty. I feel pretentious smoking them, which is a good thing because pretentious is a hell of a lot better than pathetic.

Soon I pick out Valerie's laugh in the living room. I can see her beautiful, naked body standing by the stove in my kitchen as she quietly tells me that as soon as she's had her coffee, she's going to take me down. Right there on the ceramic floor. She says, "I want you, mister" she whispers quietly. "Only you."

The thing is, Valerie didn't want me. She wanted him. And it has to do with more than pronouns. To be specific, she wanted Tony. The very next day. These details get around, then they get back to me. For this, I'm thrilled. Valerie wants Tony. I'm a stupid guy.

Yes. I know. I'm damaged goods for a long time to come. I'm wrapped in plastic and taped at weird angles.

I finish my fancy cigarette and walk home, even though Joe's expecting a ride to try and keep me at the party longer. I leave my car and walk—what must be five miles—kicking stones and putting my hands in my front pockets like it's a sad movie and I'm the star.

Down side streets, across some alleys, and then I'm on the main drag. A few dark storefronts: a dry cleaner, a laundromat, a Sicilian pizza joint that never seems to be open. The whole world feels like a ghost town now except for the All-Nite Diner. I stumble past the shadow of its neon glow. That's where Susan is—the part of the story I won't get to. There's Susan, and my future, with her green eyes, her lazy blink, that wry smile.

She's inside, ready, while I'm on the sidewalk shuffling through my gloom. I'm thinking about Valerie, about the coat I gave her, the flannel shirt, the smell of coffee, her legs and lips.

By the time I get home, I'm feeling like the useless punk my mother assured me I'd turn out to be. My feet hurt. I take off my socks and shoes and pour some vodka into my favorite glass, the old one that says Idaho. Two skiers stand beside a state map. They look the way I suppose they thought love looked back in the 1950s. They're curvy but muscleless as they smile and point toward the outline of the potato state with confidence. The woman rests her head contentedly on the man's shoulder, like they have a lovely suburban home and two kids back in Wichita, Kansas. I fill the glass up to the skiers' ankles.

As I fiddle with the radio tuner, trying to get reception for a jazz or classic rock station, it comes to me. I need a suit. I crave one. Hunter green, with slightly wider lapels than the brown suit. A suit I'll look good in even with the jacket unbuttoned. A new attitude isn't coming any time soon, but the suit is just a phone call away. I pour more vodka, no ice—up to the skiers' knees this time.

I call Lenny, turn off the saxophone solo coming from the radio and put on Hank Williams. The phone rings eight times before Lenny picks up. It's been two weeks since he dropped off the brown suit. When he answers, he sounds groggy, but I start in on how much I appreciate my brown suit. How I wore it yesterday and got compliments on the way it accented my shoulders.

"Lenny, you're amazing. I understand what you're getting at. I really do. Suits, man. Suits, Lenny. Lenny, I love you, man."

Halfway through this last sentence I realize I'm more than likely more than half drunk, but the words keep coming, and I'm not so much concentrating now on what they are as not slurring them as they come out.

"Lenny," I say. "I need a suit. Hunter green, man, hunter green."

He says, "Just a minute there, Bob. Bob? Just a minute," and he cups his hand over the receiver. This green suit has become important. I know I can never make it clear enough to Lenny.

Eventually he says, "You been drinking, Bob?"

I say, "Yes, Lenny. Yes, I have. Vodka, no ice, man. No ice."

He says, "Good. Good. I'll be over. You said green, right?"

"Right. Hunter green. Wide lapels. It's the color, man. Green. It'll change my life."

Lenny says, "Bob, you see her tonight?"

"Yes, Lenny. Valerie had on the coat I gave her for her birthday."

"Okay, Bob, okay then. You gave her a coat?"

"Yeah. Part of the reason why I'm stupid."

Eventually I give him my address, and we hang up.

The next thing I know I'm face down in my own shag carpet. Lenny rolls me over, sits me in my chair, and rummages through my drawers. I'm wondering how he got into my house, suspecting those suits might have stories to tell.

I say, "Hey, Lenny. What're you looking for in all those cupboards there?"

He says, "Coffee filters. And they're drawers. Those are cupboards. I already looked in there."

"Don't have any."

"No coffee filters?"

"No coffee. No filters. No machine. Tossed 'em. I'm supposed to be starting this wheat-free, caffeine-free, soy milk, protein-based thing. My sister's idea. She reads a lot of magazines."

Lenny holds up a plastic sack of brown rice flour. "This isn't going to work," he says.

Lenny has on a T-shirt and jeans. He looks good. European. His hair is slicked back the way I've always wanted to do mine.

He says, "You'll definitely need coffee if you're going to get measured for this thing." He motions toward the couch and the suit splayed across it in the perfect shade of green. I realize I need to take things more seriously. Lenny is a symbol, a role model, a mentor. I'm overcome with emotion and my crying turns into big heaping sobs.

Lenny busies himself with washing the dishes. The dull clink of glasses in suds makes me feel better. I'm ready to stand up. I reach for the box of Kleenex as Lenny carefully stacks my plates and bowls in the drying rack.

He says, "All ready to go, Bob?"

I follow him out my door and into the crisp late night. At the bottom of my driveway The Suit Van is waiting. The streetlight shines off Lenny's logo, a jacket on a hanger with wheels at the bottom.

We drive toward Washington Street with the windows down, cool air rushing in. I can smell earth and road and night. Every so often, I think I hear Valerie's laugh off in the distance beyond the rows of darkened houses and swaying pines. But I know that's just my head. We drive by the All-Nite Diner where I see the door gliding shut. Next week I'll stop in for a cup of coffee, a slice of pie. I'll look up and notice Susan writing out the Specials Board.

Lenny parks at a lookout point I've never known about, shifts order forms around, and plugs in the espresso maker. He messes with the coffee and then sits back in the creaky faux-leather seat, lets out a big sigh.

"Smoke?" he says.

I say, "No. No. Gave it up a few hours ago."

Lenny nods. Finally, the coffee gurgles into its little metal pot. Lenny says, "I'm getting china next week."

I sit staring at the twinkling town I live in thinking every single person understands how to make progress in this world, except me. I say, "That's really great, Lenny."

I swirl my coffee around in the cup, breathe in its deep oaky smell, and try to think seriously about my life, but I get distracted. I line events up so they make sense, and they jiggle themselves into hexagons and triangles. I say, "Lenny. You know, I think I'd be okay if I just didn't want so much decency in this world, so much fairness."

Lenny doesn't answer. He just nods. Eventually he starts up the van and says, "We've still got to get you fitted, and there's the birds chirping already."

On the way home we talk baseball scores, fishing holes, Gary and those swinging punches.

As the sun rises, Lenny crawls around on my floor with straight pins popping from his mouth, his tape measure snaking along behind. He's immaculately pressed, even now—the perfect salesman—as he slides the green jacket over my arms, tugs on a pant leg, stands back to get a good look, begins again.

Open and Shut

J ohn throws the pack of cigarettes onto the coffee table, after handing one to Sarah, taking one for himself. He flicks his silver lighter—a present from a now dead friend. He says, "You know, every time you light a cigarette it makes you sexier." He looks at her. "But only if the lighter works on the first try." He looks away. "I'll never stop smoking," he says.

Years before, John had messed up his hip in a car wreck. No one died—not even Scott, the friend who gave him the lighter—not then, not that night. Scott was the only person in the car who could stand after the wreck. He stumbled around, surveying the damage. After the creaking, shattering impact of car with ditch and then road, pitch-black-nowhere cricket-screaming Nebraska surrounded him. Scott felt fine, so he ran for help, running blind into a farmer's barbed wire fence. Then he was a cut-up mess off by himself in a field until a sleep-deprived farmer heard him. Later, it would be funny to them: the fence, Scott.

Sarah didn't know John then, hasn't known him long. He's about to walk down her stairs, out of her life. He'll say there is someone else. After that, Sarah will roll her eyes and tell him he's making a big mistake. Soon she'll ask John to hug her for just a minute on the couch, one last time. And he will. She'll try to kiss him, and he'll turn his head, say, "No. It doesn't end like that."

After John's first crash with the now dead friend, John bought an expensive sports car with the insurance settlement. A few weeks ago, when he parked near Sarah's apartment, someone stole the ashtray and some tapes from the car. Sarah lived in San Francisco for years and never once had anything stolen. John said, "Why live in this part of town? Everyone lives near 16th on the other side of O Street. This neighborhood is rough, Sarah." He told her he worried about her out here alone. Sarah told him he had better things to worry about.

Sarah lives alone and tells herself she likes it that way. She tells herself she won't let John in that far, but the simple fact is John has this smell: earth, cigarettes, leaves. Sarah's drawn to him even though he's a born-and-bred Nebraskan. Sarah wants him, and she thinks it's cool to date a cowboy, so what if he isn't really a cowboy but a film theory grad student. She likes sitting with him in her living room, smoking. It's easy. The thin air trails around the light, and the afternoon sun shifts as they talk about art and movies. Seamless. She knows that means trouble no matter how she spells it.

Sarah's heart is quiet and stubborn—numb, maybe. John is alive and naive and pretending not to be.

A month before he walks down Sarah's stairs, John drives her to his family's farm to meet his parents. His mother asks Sarah if she likes to cook. His father shows her his Victrola, a hobby, and wants to know if she eats meat. An apple pie cools on the counter. John's high school picture scowls from the wall. There's a baby cow in the barn. As John drives Sarah back to her place, the air climbing through the cracked window smells sweet. The dark feels good rippling out beyond them. The car draws a straight line on the road. For the first time Sarah isn't afraid of anything, John or the stars or the future. He holds her hand.

John lives with his ex-fiancée. He sleeps on the couch. One night they go there late because Holly, the ex-fiancée, works the third shift at a group home. It feels like stealing as John fondles her breasts on the cramped couch. Sarah runs her hands over his chest, through the coarse hair sprouting there, and thinks about infinity: fields, stars, the sky in Nebraska, skyscrapers, the ocean, salt air, the little birds darting toward and away from the water's edge. She can't stay the night. That's the deal John has with Holly—no girls overnight. Sarah doesn't mind. It seems like the normal progression of things—relationships get snags, life moves forward in fits and starts.

John's dead friend Scott was his best friend. He gave the silver lighter to John for his sixteenth birthday. For that reason, John uses it to gauge his own sexiness. John will stop smoking someday, will cease to be sexy. He'll be an old man. Sarah knows that.

Scott lived on a neighboring farm, his parents strict and religious. Once the two boys made a video mocking his preacher-father's jowl-vibrating Sunday sermon. Scott's father found it and grounded both the boys for a month even though only one of them was his son. To Sarah these stories seem old-time, like reading *Little House on the Prairie*. She can guess the endings. She knows who is good and who is bad. It's such a relief.

Back in San Francisco, before grad school on the Plains, Sarah's boyfriend Fred had a habit of walking down streets checking car doors. He'd say, "There's at least one naive fuck on every city block." One night Fred follows home two women he meets at an Urge Overkill show. Sarah says, "At least you could have called," when Fred makes it home the next day.

Fred frowns, considering the request, turns off the raging tea kettle, and says, "Why?"

"Because I was worried," Sarah says. That word, "worried" lingers in the kitchen. A cloud ready to burst.

Fred stirs sugar into his tea, tiny taps with a teaspoon. He looks at her then like he's recalibrating the tension in their relationship. Then he walks away down the hallway. "What are you?" he asks over his shoulder. "My mother?"

Eventually Sarah says, "Okay, all right, I'm overreacting." Her skin doesn't fit right. She tries to ease the tension in her stomach, stretching her arms straight out at her sides, and then up over her head. She wants to be progressive, but a wave of old-fashioned embarrassment descends as she feels old-fashioned jealousy because of these two women who crawled all over Fred. Sarah shakes it off. Fred takes her out to dinner, carries home a bundle of tulips, a bottle of wine. Sarah applies to grad school that spring.

Fred says, "Sorry babe, not going." He stretches his back by raising his hands toward the ceiling, nudging his T-shirt up above his jean's waistband. "Nebraska? They can't get any good bands out there."

"You weren't invited," Sarah says.

But that's done. That's 2,000 miles behind Sarah. She knows she needs to stay focused. It's soon after they've met. "It would be better if you didn't call my place," John says. He taps Sarah on the nose, runs a finger over her collarbone. "Holly is still pretty stuck on me." He props his boots on the trunk Sarah uses as a coffee table, says his family loves Holly. She eats meat, grew up in Omaha. What Sarah knows is that Holly has huge Midwestern breasts and red hair; she saw a bra hanging from the bathroom doorknob, a hairbrush on the kitchen counter the night she visited the apartment. Holly rushing out the door? The bra, a way to lure John back? A lacey lavender reminder?

Late one night, naked in a jumble of sheets, John tells Sarah her own breasts are the perfect size. "A hand's worth," he says, cupping each one gently. Sarah sees love in his eyes as she bites his nipples and he moans. She can't get enough. She thinks about him as she paces in front of her class, as she shops for oatmeal, orange juice, and condoms. As she vacuums.

A week before Scott died he was in John's house playing with a coat hanger talking to John's mother. Scott twisted it around and around, put it on his head like a headband to make her laugh, tossed it around a doorknob before he left. After the news of the head-on collision, John said the coat hanger was the first thing he saw.

Back in San Francisco at a dinner party, Sarah tells Fred it's time to sit down. "Dinner's ready," she whispers. "People are waiting." She asks him quietly to hold off on the drinking. Fred looks beyond her, down the hallway, out past the city limits, off into the sloppy ocean waves. He says, "Shut the fuck up." Conversation slides to a stop. Sarah smiles, frozen, burning, as Fred walks to his seat.

At home, Fred makes tea for her, kisses her on the nose when she comes through the door from work, takes off her shoes, rubs her feet. His wavy hair hangs into his eyes, curves around his small round glasses, nearly touches his soft smile. Sarah brushes the hair from his eyes, leans into him—murmurs, "You're the one, you know. You're the one for me."

Before the visit to his parents, before she'd really thought much about John, naked or otherwise, one cold, breath-biting Nebraska night, John knocks on Sarah's door, a bottle of scotch dangling from one hand, glinting in the dim light of the landing, flannel pajamas under his coat. He stands in her doorway, grinning. Happy eyes, strong, tall—the cold rushing off his body toward her. "Need a break?"

Much later, he says, "You're so beautiful." He says, "We have the most amazing sex." He says, "I love you."

Sarah does and does not believe him. It doesn't matter. The world turns on its axis. The soybeans grow at an even rate beyond the edge of town; the graduate seminars and the day-to-day maintenance of her life ticks like a clock, the second hand sweeping its face with grace and purpose.

Pouring rain, marking San Francisco winter, Sarah skips and throws her hat in the air. She's that carefree. Fred runs through puddles, full force, heavy boots spraying bouquets of rain water at his feet, hugging her, spinning—throwing his hat up and away too.

John's hip hurts when he sleeps on her futon. One day he'll walk with a cane because he refused the surgery he needed in that joint after the car wreck. Sarah says, "Lay on your back. Close your eyes." She climbs on top of him, closes her eyes, and rocks into oblivion. John is far away. She hoards him, gathers him in.

Scott, his dead friend, got hit head-on by a drunk driver, a classmate. When Sarah asks, John says, "I hate her. Everyone hated her so much she had to move away."

Sarah wonders what the woman saw on that long stretch of Nebraska road with a gentle curve at its end. What did she see right before her whole life changed? The swirling stars or just her fuzzy headlights pioneering their own way through? Was she thinking up excuses to give her parents or contemplating the new boy she'd met by the keg, the warm kiss, how he shuffled his feet and gave her shoulder a final, sweet touch?

John reads, sprawled on her couch. He says, "I've never felt this comfortable with anyone."

Sarah knows right then she'll break his heart. She smiles and says, "Me too." Not today, but already she's nostalgic, something valuable is slipping away just as it's handed to her. Her papers are scattered like giant petals at her feet. She continues typing at her tiny desk, but she feels John, knows he's watching her. Out the window, the neighbor's dog sniffs the sidewalk, barks at the leaves. The sun dapples across her face. Sarah turns toward him; her mind on nothing else.

The last Halloween before she leaves the city for good, Fred dresses as a pervert: Sarah's too-tight pants padded in the crotch to look like a hard-on, gold chains, unbuttoned polyester shirt, blackened teeth, greased stringy hair. At the party, he rubs against people, flips them off. Everybody laughs, slaps him on the back. Sarah dresses as a man dressed as a woman: tight black fringy dress, black silk hose, black pumps, bright red lips, bushy mustache. She carefully manicures five o'clock shadow onto her cheeks, pulls an antique velvet hat down to her eyes. She floats above the crowds in the street, a spy, undercover. Later, her mustache falls into her beer. Drunk and tired, she stumbles home by herself, calves cramping from the heels, happy to slip into a T-shirt, crawl into bed. Fred stays until dawn for the dancing, the pot brownies.

On their first date, John takes her to a park for a picnic lunch. A fountain and blue sky. Sarah loves that he knows about these secret spots. The old park hidden in a residential neighborhood has a rusty fence stretched full of vines. It feels like she's in an English garden. The cherub waterfall trickles, and sunlight spills through the delicate branches of the trees. Across town, they push into a bar and play pinball, order a pitcher of beer. Already Sarah leans into John, touches him, drawn to him, his flesh, the mass that makes him up: sun, soil, grains. She doesn't know what it is in him that draws her in, but she can't help herself, diving deeper—even years later the thought of him makes her shudder. She asks him in, stays up all night talking about San Francisco, her friends, the ocean, the restaurants, the streets at night, the energy, the pace.

In San Francisco, Sarah likes to be alone—alone with someone. That's what she says when friends ask; she wants to take off and not call. She likes not being missed or needed. It makes life easier. Life with Fred, Sarah says, is the perfect relationship.

One day her friends June and Kriscinda pull up beside Sarah standing at the train stop. Sarah is headed to the library to return books, reading voraciously to bone up for graduate school. June leans out the window, "I knew that was you. Only Sarah could pull off a plaid with a flower print. C'mon, stop being a geek and be a sexy babe with us."

Sarah jumps into the car and then sits with them on the windy beach smoking cigarettes and scowling at the men who look their way. Kriscinda says, "So what are you and Fred doing about the relationship? Long distance or what?"

Sarah mentions low-maintenance, being alone. She's going to grad school to get serious about herself. "Fuck guys," she says, "I'm sick of them."

June adjusts her perfect breasts in her J. Crew bikini. "I know," she says, "The next guy I get serious about is going to be the one. I mean, for life. With babies. I'm tired of fucking around." She hugs her knees, "Don't you wish we could just do this every day? You know, just hang with the girls," June asks. "Except we'd miss orgasms. Sarah, won't you miss orgasms?"

Sarah smiles. "Orgasms," she says, tipping her head back as the light glitters in her sunglasses, makes her red lipstick sparkle. "Orgasms are little tricksters that get us into trouble."

"Let's swim," Kriscinda says. And they jump up and run toward the water. Sarah pulls off her dress. As she races toward the first tiny wave in black underwear and bra, she wonders if they're imitating joy or actually experiencing it. Splashing into the cold water, screaming, she thinks she will miss the sex a little bit.

Arriving in Nebraska for the first time late at night, Sarah dozes uneasily in her hotel room worrying about what she will see when she wakes up. She drove from San Francisco to witness every mile of the way. It's July, hot and humid. She kept the car windows down, her T-shirt sleeves rolled up.

Before she pulls away from the curb in front of her old apartment, Kriscinda hugs her hard, says the key to traveling is reapplication of lipstick. "A girl has to look good on the road." She presses a tube of Real Raisin into her palm. "Nebraska. Sarah?

You're going to eat them alive." Sarah nods, teary-eyed, gets in and turns the key to her Tercel.

June leans her head in. "There might not be espresso, you know. Let me know what you need. I'll FedEx it. We'll watch Fred for you," she says. "We'll keep an eye on him." Fred is a silhouette in the bay window. He waves once, blows a kiss, and disappears. June pats the hand Sarah clenches around the wheel. "The other thing is sunglasses." June carefully adjusts a pair of cat-eye frames over Sarah's ears. A big breath, and Sarah puts the car into gear before she can change her mind.

John wants to give her a kitten from his parents' farm. "Every so often," he says, "there's one that stands out from the others." He's afraid this one will get run over by a tractor or stepped on by a cow. Sarah says no way. But she does know a woman, Dawn, in her Edith Wharton seminar, who's looking for a kitten. She left her boyfriend and wants a pet to rely on for unconditional love. The little tiger cat is curled in a corner of the barn, asleep. It's a purring ball of electricity by the time they pull up in front of Dawn's house. "I feel like I've wound it up. Now I'm afraid to let it go," Sarah says. Dawn planned a Welcome Home party for the kitten she'd already named Neil.

Sarah helps Dawn make drinks in the kitchen. When she pokes her head into the living room, John and a woman from her art history class, Tereneh, are dangling a piece of yarn above Neil's outstretched paw, laughing. Later, Sarah rubs John's ankle. They share a bowl of ice cream.

In San Francisco as Fred snores softly beside her, Sarah stares at the city lights swirling around their ceiling, wondering if this is all okay, if this is what her life is going to be like, forever.

John whispers, "I'm trying to give you love," as he slides inside her. "Do you understand that? I'm trying to give you love."

John has a photograph of Scott, grinning from ear to ear, an arm draped around his girlfriend's shoulder. She died that night too. On impact. John seems slighted because of this, like Scott's girlfriend should have been alive to mourn with him. Sarah thinks it's romantic, in a way—young love frozen at the moment of impact. When she says this to John, he just stares at her, blinking.

"So you're just going away? You guys haven't talked?" Kriscinda stirs her chai tea, blows smoke into the air and fans it away. She cut her bangs too short and keeps pulling at them as if they'll grow on the spot.

"No, we haven't said a thing," Sarah says. "He knows he needs to get a new apartment, that I'm driving there by myself, but I guess as far as the relationship goes it'll just work itself out." Sarah looks out the coffee shop's large plate glass window. It's always beautiful in San Francisco, always spring, always exciting—or she'll always remember it that way. Sarah doesn't know why she needs to get out, but she does. The man across 16th Street lines up lemons and limes at the produce market. The guy behind the counter at Café Macondo puts on a salsa tape.

Kriscinda says, "Well. It's obvious to everyone Fred adores you. I just don't know what you think of him half the time."

Sarah looks at her. "I'm really going to miss you."

"Oh, honey, you'll be back. What're you going to do? Marry a cowboy? Anyway, think of all the great thrift stores you'll find. You can ship us stuff and we'll resell it for bucketloads."

When John picks her up that day for their first date, they're both playing the same cassette tape—John in his car, Sarah in her apartment. Sarah has never believed in fate, but suddenly there's a click of bigger, richer meaning, like a lighter lit on the first try.

Before they moved to San Francisco, back in Vermont Sarah and Fred met through an ex-boyfriend who'd introduced them by saying, "Now here are two people who could really fuck each other up." Sarah thought Fred was interesting but too short for her. She could never be with a short man, she told her ex.

The next month in Boston, a local funk band played as Fred danced up to her and said, "Hey babe, need a sugar daddy? You know, someone to take care of you—all of your needs?" He laughed at her expression and said, "Want another beer?"

After a few weeks of movies and coffee and beer at the bar near her apartment, as they rolled around in Sarah's bed, she said, "So, are we going to have sex?"

Fred said, "I think that would be beautiful."

Sarah laughed. It was corny, naive, like a cliché. It couldn't simply be beautiful for two people who'd met on a dance floor soaked in beer. Fred had a condom buttoned into his jean jacket pocket. They came at the same time.

"Cool," he said.

Sarah said, "Yeah, cool." They lay together until morning, not talking or sleeping, just waiting for their future to begin.

Sarah wants to hear stories about farming, about what it's like growing up in the middle of nowhere. John tries, but Sarah can tell he doesn't really know what it's like. He's still right in the middle of it.

One day, John is late, frazzled when he shows up at Sarah's house. He'd been talking about Žižek with Tereneh in her studio. He hugs Sarah, smiles. In the car, they zoom and zig through slow moving traffic, stop at a bar for french fries and beer, sit together on the same side of the booth, Sarah's hand resting on his thigh.

When Fred leaves San Francisco for a vacation with his parents, Sarah calls Bob. He's a long-term temporary office worker/drummer she met on a short-term temp assignment. He's charming and clever—available, and he loves to dance.

Sarah and Bob frequent a small bar a couple of blocks down Haight Street, packed with older hipsters, not the squeaky-new, pretentious ones. Everyone looks interesting to Sarah. She wonders why she doesn't have more friends.

They're drinking whiskey straight. Bob names the drink, "The Working Class." He wants the name to catch on. "We'll have two Working Classes," he says, as Sarah mouths, "Whiskey, straight up." The bartender nods.

"Hey, have you noticed that everyone in San Francisco pretends they don't have a job? You know, it's so uncool to just be doing okay. You have to be down-and-out," Bob says.

Sarah smiles. She says, "Like you have to be seen having breakfast on a weekday so you can let people know you work part-time. Or you have to be a temp so you can say it's only a temporary thing."

"Right, the down-and-out syndrome. If you get a full-time job all your friends dump you because you're so square you can't go to Ocean Beach to play Frisbee. We've got it too, you know." Bob grins, his eyes small sharp hyphens, "Let's be down-and-out together, okay?"

"Okay, but I think you need to slouch more. You look like you've got forty hours under your belt, maybe even health coverage."

"Yeah, but I've got the right drink, right? That's half of it. I'm all working class down-and-out tonight."

When the next song comes on, Bob pulls Sarah onto the dusty floor. Sarah knows even if Bob says he doesn't want to have sex with her—his body does. They're caught there in that mood, in that sexy city, down-and-out desperation on their minds. The song ends, and they look at each other, sweaty with electricity.

"Fred never wants to come dancing," Sarah says. "He only likes to go to shows where they stand perfectly still with toilet paper shoved into their ears."

Bob laughs, "Yeah, I know. He's mister post-punk."

"Down-and-out post-punk, that is."

Bob is a nice guy. Sarah knows they'll only sleep together if she leaves Fred, but she can't leave because that would mean giving up the curved bay windows of their apartment, the in-house laundry, the joint checking account. Sarah can't give up on Fred, but Bob is her world as she follows him up his staircase, sits talking with him on his bed.

John asks, "Do you think we'll ever live together?"

Sarah says, "There won't ever be a house big enough, not enough rooms. Never, ever. I'm living alone for the rest of my goddamn life. I know how men are."

"Oh, and how's that?" John asks, a hurt look flitting across his face as he turns away from her, clicking on her TV and reaching for a cigarette.

"Men keep things. They always score, so here I am about $2,000 lighter than I should be, without my tennis racket, the deco standing lamp, my 35 mm camera, the phone chair, my stereo, all of my albums, countless shirts, jeans, and jackets. Here I am living alone."

Later, at Pho Tau Bay, a Vietnamese restaurant on 27th with a glass storefront facing the busy street, Sarah pretends she's in a bustling city with traffic and bright lights. Sipping small cups of super-sweet Vietnamese coffee at a wobbly table, the streetlights pop on. The owner's daughter folds napkins in the corner, surrounded by empty plastic chairs.

John says, "Want to go see a band at the Hurricane?"

Sarah pulls her chair closer to him. "No, not really. I want to see you. Want to see me? Are we seeing each other? Are we going steady?" Sarah kisses his nose. She loves his nose and his eyes, so dark and steady. Safe. A car zips by the plate glass window. The streetlights cast an eerie glow.

Sarah has never had a friend die. It's always a friend's friend. The friend turns to her when they don't want to think about death anymore, and she takes them for long walks on the beach. As they walk, talk slowly turns to hair color or nail polish, mahogany highlights or Gunmetal Gray enamel. Talk is small again, death and fairness on the back burner for a few good hours.

Kriscinda dyes her hair four times as her friend Shayne edges toward his slow, silent death. She gets it cut ten times. She calls it, "re-styling." Her last style is a buzz cut in neon red. Kriscinda says it's the only option she hasn't tried. Sarah takes her to an arcade where they pose like old movie stars in the photo booth. A few days later, Kriscinda shows up on her doorstep. "Shayne is dead, and I look ridiculous." Sarah pulls Kriscinda inside. She hugs her and says the only thing she knows to say: "Jet black and a bottle of Jim Beam?"

Kriscinda laughs and then cries.

"Fritos too. We'll get Fritos."

Later that night, Fred says, "You guys smoke too much."

"Nope, we don't. Under the circumstances, we're doing just fine."

"It's a disgusting habit." He walks away into the kitchen. Sarah smiles. She refuses to stop even though Fred can no longer see her. Fred yells in, "I'm not kissing you with that smoke breath."

Sarah whispers, "Yippee!" She turns to watch the sunset out their window, burnt sienna, glowing, heaving itself up to take a big inhale.

John will tell her they need to talk. He'll touch her knee and look at her with sad, velvety eyes, smooth skin, freckles. He'll say, "It's Tereneh. I guess you know that."

If Scott hadn't died, he would have joined the fraternity with John that first year, a geeky farmer's fraternity John is embarrassed to talk about. They would have rushed together, gotten bombed, and flirted with all the big-haired sorority girls dancing to "Brick House." John knows his whole life would be different if Scott hadn't died.

Fred's urban eccentricities are insecurities. He laughs when people do embarrassing things, kicks cars if they stop mid-cross-walk. When he gets drunk in a crowded bar he talks about his ex-girlfriends' breasts.

Sarah says, "So what's your ex-fiancée like, anyway?"

John says, "Oh, Holly just wanted to be my wife, you know. That's all. I couldn't take that pressure. And her hair. It's red and curly and just all wrong."

"Oh, I see," Sarah says, as they speed through the afternoon. John has named the grains growing in the fields alongside the road. Sarah watches heads of milo watching her watch them. Like watching an ocean. Waves cresting. She says, "Her hair. Now there's a good, rational reason to break off a marriage plan."

Sarah started reading Fred's journal back when they first met. That's how she knew he wanted to travel with her and move

45

to San Francisco, that he was falling in love with her but knew she would dump him some day. Sarah saw it as a challenge. She'd stay with Fred if it killed her. Fred called himself a loser late at night as they lay in bed listening to their neighbors listening to The Smiths. Sarah tried to convince him otherwise. By the time they made it to San Francisco and their first apartment, she had grown bored with his journal entries. He often left the little black book in obvious places, but Sarah stopped taking the bait, preferring a life with Fred where she didn't know what was coming.

John says, "I'll be so excited when Holly leaves so you can come over and stay at my place."

"Really? When's she leaving?"

"December."

"Yeah. That'll be nice. We can take turns sleeping over. Why didn't you just move out when you broke off the engagement?"

"She didn't believe me, and I felt bad for her."

"Oh, that's nice."

"She thought I'd get over it, that it was just a phase. But really, she grosses me out."

A week passes, Sarah doesn't hear from John, except late one night, a phone call from a bar.

He says, "I was just kidding around about being a free and easy guy." Bar noises surge, and there's static around each word.

Sarah asks if she can meet them at the bar. She can hear someone in the background yell, "Yeah, Sarah, get your ass down here." But John says he thinks they'll be leaving soon. Sarah just wants to be near him for a little while. She says, okay, that he can stop by later. She says it would be more than okay to stop by.

Kriscinda's voice pops out from the answering machine as

Sarah bolts from bed, runs down the hall to grab it before she hangs up. "Hey, babe."

"Hey, cool. Sorry it's so early for you, but I'm never home when the normal budget phone time is going. I wanted to check on the progress on the Plains. How's the cowboy?"

Sarah yawns, props her feet on the windowsill, lays on her back. The apartment and the street are silent. The sky is dark edging toward morning as a few birds sleepily chirp. Sarah misses the buzzing, beeping horns in the city, the sound of the homeless people sorting through the curbside recycling bin below her and Fred's bedroom window, glass bottles clattering and a rickety shopping cart rolling along the sidewalk. Kriscinda smokes on the other end of the receiver, a short intake of breath and then the gushing of her words as she exhales.

"Any cool new finds?"

"There's this huge chicken outside this fried chicken place here. It's called Lee's Chicken. The statue is gigantic—postcard material, I think. But the best thing is the blind organ player. When I walked in, she was playing the Barney theme song."

"No shit?"

"She sings too. And there are all these stoic Nebraskans just chewing their chicken. It was very, very surreal. The downside is that all I could eat was a baked potato and a side salad. And you know, the cowboy? Well, I really think he might be the one. I really feel like I'm falling for him. I really think he could be molded into the perfect guy if I just migrated him over to the city."

"Well, cool. Did I mention Christopher is moving out?"

"I've heard it before. He won't pull through."

"No really this time he has a departure date. He has a plane ticket. He says he's tired of hurting me. I'm really about to lose it even though he's been threatening this disaster for years."

Kriscinda's crying is tiny through the stiff plastic receiver, traveling all the miles between them. After the parade of relationships, as time passes and people die and everyone grows older, here they are just as lost as ever. Sarah says, "So, what comes next?"

"Oh, I don't know. I'm definitely going to lose the apartment. Is it time for the nunnery or the asylum? There are so many options for a strong, stunning woman like me."

"Hmmm. I think they'd have better food in the nunnery, and it'd probably be easier to sneak out. The uniforms and early morning hours would be unbearable though. Why don't you move to Nebraska? Meet a cowboy?"

"Not happening, Sarah. Not happening. Way too flat. I've seen the postcards. How do people end relationships these days? What did you say to Fred?"

"Bad example. Nothing."

"Nothing?"

"I didn't even tell him about the new cowboy. I just said, 'Let's date other people.'"

"Well, what'd he say?"

He said, "You're such a mature woman."

"Fuck."

"Yeah. Hell if I know. How do you break up when you had an open relationship to begin with? It just doesn't seem worth the emotion. Plus, he has my stereo. I really want my stereo back. He still calls me every week, and each time he gets more boring. How many rockabilly bands can there be in the world?"

"You don't want to know."

They laugh. Kriscinda sniffles, lights another cigarette. Outside the big Nebraska sky starts to unwrap itself. Sarah hears a truck start. Her neighbor opens his door to let the dog out. It barks twice at the crisp fall air. "What's it like there right now, Kris?"

"It's three a.m. Let's see." Sarah can hear Kriscinda's window as it slides up. "Let's see who knows what it's like here." Wind ruffles into the receiver. Kriscinda yells, "Hey you. Hey. What's it like here? Yeah, what's it like?"

"It's fucking beautiful!" comes forward from the staticky background. Kriscinda slams the window shut. "There you have it."

John is the sound of footsteps. He is the apartment door as it clicks shut. Sarah is the couch and the window and the dark, startling night.

Nebraska Men

I n Nebraska, men keep small colorful seashells in their
mouths. When they speak, which isn't often, the soft
roar of the ocean hums behind each word. In this way they are able
to understand each distant coast. They are able to look across their
long, flat fields and imagine ships rocking slowly to port, see each
grain ripening earnestly in the Midwestern sun, see time moving
slowly in a line toward a very specific day.

The men stop and take their hats from their heads. They
squint and whistle quiet tunes to songs they never knew. They
smile. At night they ease their warm bodies into crisp white beds;
they slowly rub their wives' backs. The men make soft circles with
their rough hands and are gentle as winter wheat. Just as the women
are about to sleep, they say goodnight to them; they kiss them softly.

When they wake, the men smile and say good morning to
no one in particular, to their sleeping wives' tousled hair, to the

mist clearing. They are quiet as they get out of bed, walk down their stairs. Nebraska men understand three a.m. and cows. It is their job.

When they get thirsty, they shift the shells to a soft hollow pocket that has formed in their cheeks. This gesture makes the smallest noise, barely audible over the whimper of a dog, the cottonwood leaves. The men turn on the faucet that is beside their sturdy graying barn. The water streams out in a high screech; they tilt their heads, stretch their thick red tongues.

It is then that the men come face-to-face with every single day in the year. They think how the one they're living today is no better than the last, how the next could possibly be the best one of all.

Silent Chickens

T apping, tapping, tapping. They do it all night long, those plump little monsters. *Tap. Tap.* I can't hear them from my bedroom window—with the breeze blowing the curtains out like a school girl's hair and my cup of tea weighing so heavy in my sweaty palm.

My cat parades, stampedes, through the kitchen, then the living room, then the kitchen again. She's a herd of mustangs out on the open prairie. She is a ticker-tape parade.

There should be bells chiming, but they haven't met their cue.

I can't hear the chickens, but I know they're down there.

Tapping.

II

Simple

L ate one night Butch told her the first word he ever said was *pretty*. The word floated lightly on the evening air. It managed to lace itself around Nicole's heart in a way that made her turn on her side and say, "That's the sweetest thing I've ever heard."

Butch curled himself closer, drawing her long legs through his, tangling their lives like two floating fishnets. He ran his hand through her long hair while he told her stories. Stories about moons rising, like the one outside her bedroom window, rising slowly like a dandelion ready to blow away and leave the night pitch-black and lonely—moons waiting for lovers like themselves to make the darkness into something more.

Butch said they were in love. He said it more than once. But they were only a man and a woman telling stories in the bedroom of a second-floor apartment with a moon there confusing everything.

In a month he's gone, vanished, like a moonlit dandelion in a windy field. Nicole stands in her second-story window watching cars pass, watching the birdbath's water lie still and untouched.

The world is large and looming. It rotates on the same axis as the lighted pie display at the All-Nite Diner on the corner of her street. Coconut cream, pecan, chocolate, and blueberry. Nicole watches layer cake, Jell-O, and tapioca. She knows there are choices she can't even see yet—ideas she can't understand. When the waitress comes, Nicole orders coffee. She stirs it slowly as she tells the woman she needs a few more minutes to decide. Nicole watches the sleepy street waiting for the noisy morning. For now, she sees only her own hazy reflection telling her to decide soon—to pick something, anything.

Months later with the moon through the window it's as if Butch is there with her again. Nicole hates herself, but it happens. He comes spinning into her memory, a tornado she hasn't heard about in the weather reports. He touches down.

It's a summer night. Nicole's window is open. No breeze billows her thin white curtains. She can't sleep. It's a dark insomnia. "Pretty, my ass," she mumbles to the gaping closet, to her sleeping cat, to the empty space beside her in bed.

Nicole fingers a book of Italian poetry another man has recently given her. She thinks about another lover years before who took her swimming in Vermont and kissed her as they stood fighting the rapids.

As the moon comes into view, hanging in between branches, she feels Butch pulling at her—pulling as if they could never be close enough.

Butch is with another woman, Judy, years later now, in another state, a different time and place—in a sparkling apartment seventeen floors up from the honking city streets. It's winter. They're on a leather couch, heads resting against one another.

Butch touches Judy's hand and says, "Hey, did you know the first word I ever said was *pretty*?"

The television mumbles softly. Two empty wine glasses rest on the floor along with the empty bottle of red that has fallen on its side. One slow drop will stain the carpet as Judy replies.

She lifts her head to look at Butch with a wry smile. She pushes her long hair to the side and says, "Really? That's so pretentious."

She laughs then and pushes on his forehead so she can lean her head back onto his shoulder.

Butch looks out the window at the ragged skyline of a city he has come to know too well. He feels boredom hovering in the corners again. He feels the cold snap diving in and scratching at his bones.

Breezy floating drapes rise into Butch's thoughts; there's a cat jumping from a windowsill onto a black trunk; a face then it's gone.

Butch nudges Judy. He whispers that they should go to bed; they should turn off the TV and have sweet dreams back in the bedroom. He kisses her on the forehead.

Judy nods and smiles, half asleep. They shuffle to the back bedroom, forgetting the TV. It blinks a hazy blue-gray late into the night.

The next morning when Butch gets up early to make coffee he thinks he hears Nicole whispering in the kitchen. But it's just the TV.

Czechoslovakia

As we rode the train, the bumpy, whirling train, to that small enchanting town, it was like riding a live bumblebee. Fast and furious with clanking metal and yellow-and-black seats. The sun was rising, and you awkwardly put your arm around my shoulder and pulled me close. You did this because you knew I wanted you to. It continued to be awkward the whole way there to that town filled with black-and-white tiled floors and boisterous pubs filled with missing teeth and large bosoms, hairy knuckles and dark brown pants.

Once there I told you about doing it on top of my mom's washing machine when I was fourteen years old—back in the back room of the remodeled basement. Back among dusty canning jars and rusty Campbell's soup. The smell of Downy and Tide, the sagging plastic clothes basket and the pile of clean towels. You told me to stop, that you were getting excited, but I couldn't—that was the problem.

And the next morning in the bleak, ancient cemetery, we practiced saying "Hello there" in every different accent and language we knew. You walked fast, ten feet ahead of me, shouting over your shoulder like you were from Oklahoma, Italy, and Germany—arms flapping and pushing forward against a low gray sky. I ran behind: Nebraska, Wyoming, California. Stumbling on the rocky ground, laughing.

And as I boarded the sighing train again, but alone, we assured each other we would see each other again soon, and it would be the same, and we would be in something, if not love.

House

E ven the dogs here are old. They shuffle up and down
the steep streets, one paw barely leading the others.
They sniff the sidewalk with disinterest and blink their clouded
cataract eyes as I pass.

I have this place, a house where it's quiet as night descends, where I peek out the window like a suspicious widow
expecting the worst.

I ran away long ago. It's okay to run. It's just the stopping
that hurts. It's just that it's so very quiet.

At night the tomcats howl. When they start, they screech
and gurgle like newborns. Sometimes I imagine someone has left a
child for me out there lying in the gutter. But the moon rises and the
howls descend to moans. It's then that I know no child is there. There
is just lust and air and the cat's sharp, keen claws with the sound of
metal as he makes his leap off the garden fence to creep away.

I Have This System for Getting Exactly What I Want Out of People

I make dinner. Roast something dark and sweet, a beef roast, some beets. The whole house embraces the smell of intrigue. The creak of the oven door. The glug of red wine.

I hug. I cheek kiss, twice. Graciousness with an apron. The people, my friends, enter with some caution but then settle into themselves—their drinks, the cheeses and crisp bread. They can't help it. They cross ankles and chat in small groups. Tip-tapping, waiting.

I smile, my lips quivering. I try to push that down, the nerves. Think about confidence and a kind of ending that won't make me look bad. And then everyone takes a seat. They jumble into chairs with napkins unleashed. More wine. And just as the group has their forks poised in left and right hands, just as they raise them up to dig in, the sweet smell of all my work flaring their nostrils, just then I clear my throat, remind them of our friendship, of their faithfulness over the years.

You can see their eyes glaze a bit, their jaws take on a firm line.

"What do you want, DeeAnn?" Jacob asks, pushing at his sleeves. "You always have these nice dinners and then people get in fights and stomp off."

"Not always," I say. "Sometimes everything goes smoothly. Sometimes we make it to dessert. Remember last July? Dessert on the screened-in porch?"

Jacob sighs, takes a quick bite of the beef as if he wants to get something out of the night before it goes to hell. Megan snaps up a beet. Naomi tops off her wine so it's a tiny red lake hovering above the white tablecloth.

"I need for all of you to work harder," I say, smiling, tapping my nails against the side of my plate. These beautiful plates that a friend supplied years before and insisted I keep. That was back when people understood generosity. How was I to suspect those kindnesses could end?

"Harder?" Megan says. "At what?" She tears off a large piece of baguette. Looks to Jacob for reassurance.

"I mean, what have you done for me lately?" My question falls feebly into a newly formed pocket of silence.

"How much wine, DeeAnn? How much wine did you drink before we arrived? I want to understand where we are here," Jacob says. "Are you going to throw a tantrum? Why do we even try with you?"

Troy, Naomi's boyfriend—new to our circle—pushes his chair back a little, glances at his wristwatch.

"Because you love me," I say. The obvious answer, obviously. I extend my arms as if to encompass the table. "Because you enjoy helping. You do. All of you. Because I make you amazing food and house-sit your pets and remember your children's names. I do all this stuff, and all I ask is that you listen to me right now."

"Work harder," Naomi says. She smiles, nodding. Naomi likes to get things right.

"Yes, exactly," I say. "Harder."

"Okay. I'll chop some wood later," Naomi says and rests her hands in her lap. "Can I have dessert?"

"Yes."

"Dishes," Megan says without conviction. "But I did the dishes last time we were here, and it kind of sucked."

"Then don't volunteer, Megan," Jacob says. "Don't do things you don't want to do for DeeAnn because chances are you won't hear from her for months after this, anyway. You'll wait. You'll call, but she won't return your calls. Will you, DeeAnn?" Jacob nabs the serving spoon, heaps on a large smattering of garlic mashed potatoes with fresh chives.

"I'll screw you, DeeAnn," he says. "Even though I did that last time and even though it also kind of sucked." Jacob addresses the table as he speaks, his eyes roving to me and then to the empty wine bottles, and then back to me like a well-thrown dart.

"You get what you ask for, don't you, dear?" Judy, Jacob's ex says to me, clutching her knife, which still holds a smudge of butter.

Rise and Settle Again

Words stretch out like a clothesline as Ellen reads a book in the yard. Thoughts of Jack sweep in like tides as she turns each page. She has questions she can never ask him. They drive her outside into the early evening light.

Ellen has taken to observing their home from afar, the dog at her side. After a while, the dog sighs, then wanders off to gnaw a stick.

Ellen daydreams of dusting for fingerprints as she rubs a blade of grass, tips her head to the coming dusk. Cool air skirts beneath the hot and down the hillside. She rearranges her thighs in the metal chair as the light turns silver-gray.

Jack's truck door slams. He rambles up the walk, snakes toward the front door. She can see it all from her vantage point, slightly elevated in the sloped backyard. Their front door opens, closes.

Ellen knows Jack will make his way through the house. He'll glance at the stack of dirty dishes, push his hand through his hair. He'll strip naked—probably right there in the kitchen, a new thing, walking naked through the house. It makes Ellen think of kings, of courts and jesters, the way his chest puffs out. His penis swaying. Jack will pour a drink, read the paper, eat leftovers—anything—naked.

She hears the shower start up. The radio turned low. The dog's ears perk and he bangs his tail against the ground, runs to the back screen door, looks expectantly at the dark within.

Ellen lets the mosquitoes settle upon her, rise and settle again. A light glows—a tiny speck from the house's interior. By the time Jack makes it out to the yard pitch-black has tumbled in.

When they met Jack and Ellen sparked like flint. Eyes lit up at the party, then the bar, then walking hand in hand to breakfast in the cool morning air. Everything slid together and fit right. That day, they looked in unison at the bird on the wire, the hobby store's window display, the line of parking meters that stretched to infinity—their metal heads nodding along block after block. Ellen leaned her head into his shoulder; Jack cupped her waist.

And it isn't his fault as much as his destiny to push everything away, to work too hard and drink too hard. To fight sometimes, late at night at the bar. He works and works and works until he loses sight of himself and makes his way home to her.

But by then Ellen is adrift in the yard or at the kitchen table with a magazine, stiff and frozen and waiting, just waiting for things to change.

Jack opens the back door, makes his way up the crooked sidewalk, sits on the grass beside her, reaches up to tap her knuckle. To hold a finger, to touch her hand.

And Then

Sitting drunk on the musty couch on the screened-in porch. The night noises come clunking in. A train. Night construction down far away on the highway. Moist plants—the smell of tomatoes and marigolds seeps in from the yard.

It's all there.

The collection of glasses I've placed on a shelf—lined up like soldiers. They glow the longer my drunk prevails.

And then he comes in—the lover who isn't so fresh and new anymore. The lover whose habits have become, well, air. The life merging with mine. He comes with the bottle of wine. It's the second bottle—the same as years before with another lover who has since become the memory of a second bottle of wine, late at night.

We're drunk, lulling ourselves into one another. No surprises. And there's the cat. Curled up and purring for once—for once a saint of a cat. No tearing up curtains or clawing at the door like a prize fighter. Just purring, curled with her sides expanding like little bellows.

And he looks out into the dark night, looks at the cat, looks at me with his eyes matching the sparkling city lights we can't see from here. He sits down, hand sliding slowly onto my knee, cat in-between. There's a patient stretch of silence.

"I love this cat," he suddenly says, arms extended toward the cat's incomprehensible face.

It's a night of miracles. He doesn't love the cat, although he has tried. And, as if in a brief act of gratitude, the cat purrs louder.

I stare at the glass collection some more—the way the outdoor sounds combine with the candle flickering on the table—off the glass, the glass, the glass.

He says, "I love you." He snuggles into me then, like a boy, and I nestle him in like the son I'll never have.

And the cat is nudged from its half-sleep and walks patiently to the kitchen to crunch food. She will stick her paw into her water bowl and lick—paw-lick-paw-lick.

Everything sways and then returns in my head. And I'm in love. There, that night, as much as I possibly know how to be—bursting at the seams love—suddenly, without preamble.

And the sounds go on, and the sky is falling in, and happiness seems possible—pure, sweet, uncluttered.

Now

The coffee shop is full, or full enough. I hide in the back, wait. My maybe-date doesn't show. "The alarm clock didn't go off," he says to me when he calls. To get to the coffee shop on time, I sprinted through my morning, brushed my teeth like a comedy routine, threw on clothes, made hasty decisions, pissed off the dog and the cat and my neighbor, Jim. But still. I'm polite on the phone, as maybe-date talks about late nights and the need for a new, better alarm clock.

I doubt the problem is the clock, but I encourage him to, yes, buy a new one. I say it's okay, because it seems he will not stop apologizing until I do. I hate that I'm bullied into forgiving him, and when he calls to reschedule I pretend I've accidentally deleted his message.

I take joy where I can. These tiny moments I create add up. As I'm walking my dog I think about all the missed opportunities, all the rushing. What if you got that back—a time refund?

And today in fact, there's almost-date sitting in a different coffee shop talking to a different woman as I walk by. I turn, walk by again. I turn, walk to the window and tap. *Tap, tap.* Wave. He looks up, touches the woman's hand to stop her mid-sentence, nods to me, and then heads out into the cold without a coat. I'm bundled tight. The dog sits, sensing this will be a long one, deciding to be a good boy for a change, and the possibility of a treat.

"Hey," almost-date says. "I tried calling you to hook up again."

"Oh, hey," I say. "I didn't get that message. Weird."

"Weird," he says. We both look at the dog, who looks across the street, his main focus being sitting like a good boy. Shoulders just so.

I look inside at the woman with her back to me, sipping on a cup of tea, fiddling with the paper flag attached to the string attached to her tea bag. Her fingers are fine and beautiful. Her hair looks nice from the back, auburn, wavy, lush. I wonder how many people he has in his life. I feel homesick for something I can't quite define.

He looks through the coffee shop window, perhaps thinks the woman's hands are beautiful too. Maybe this is the moment that he falls in love with her? In a few years they'll marry, this man and the woman with the tea. They'll walk arm in arm around the neighborhood and smile at me in the dwindling light. They'll get a dog of their own. A beagle who will sniff my dog's butt.

For now, my dog has decided his good dog time is up. He whines a little and then lifts off his haunches and pulls gently on the leash.

"Okay," the man says. He sighs then, looks across the street at the rows of houses lined up and quiet in the midafternoon city light, their window boxes stuffed with dying flowers. He says, "I've seen you around this neighborhood for months. I always thought it was beautiful, the way you walk so carefully with your dog. I love that you smiled at me the first time we passed each other," he says. "Just wanted to let you know that." He shifts his weight from one foot to the other, touches my arm.

I nod. I say, "Thank you." The dog pulls steadily now and barks once. I say, "Thanks."

I think about all of this later, of course. I think about time stretching and bending and moving. I imagine the woman waiting patiently while conversations inside the coffee shop murmur and spin all around her, as the woman turns to look out the window to see me with him.

The Bridge

Once again Jim digs into his pocket to show us the thin piece of metal attached to his apartment keys.

"I built that bridge," he says. And we nod. That famous smoky orange suspension breathing across the bay. "I built it," he says again.

Even then, we could tell the days were numbered at O'Leary's bar. Maybe that's why we settled there more and more. Perched on bar stools in the dim light, we searched for something we couldn't have. We sensed the flickering, the near-extinction of the place, our youth in contrast.

The Irish bartender, cheeks a ruddy red, a puff of eyebrow-mustache-sideburn, never spoke a word. We pointed to the keg tap, he poured, counted change from the dollars we kept on the bar.

We huddled in the corner. Most of the place went unused every night, except for the once-a-year St. Patty's celebration with a band and food and crepe paper clovers, all lit up.

Most days though it was just Dick and Jim and Margaret. Margaret with her stuffed animals lined up in a row. Toothless Margaret who sweetly crooned harmony to Dick and his guitar. He sang the old country songs we loved, "Sioux City Sue" and "T for Texas" and, when we begged, "I'm So Lonesome I Could Cry." Dick said he didn't like to sing the sad songs. When we asked why, Dick just set down his guitar and sipped from his glass like we weren't there. So we stopped asking.

When everything got going just right Jim pulled out his harmonica. And then, some nights, the key chain.

What he couldn't tell us about was the open world he'd seen—the time before the bridge was there. The yawn of nothing that he and a thousand other men filled with their bare hands.

Every worker on that bridge got a link on his key chain. How many women had asked if they could keep it? How many crazy friends had tried to pocket it? He kept that little chunk of metal that put him up there in the clouds lacing together the mountains, stitching up the shores. The crisp expanse of water. The boats sliding through like bugs. The horizon rising and falling in stark shadows. Early morning sounds smacking the shoreline, as the birds stretched their wings and took flight.

Wyoming

I n Wyoming, baby cows are born with fluffy white clouds for faces. Birds fall fast and furious from the sky. They don't get hurt. It's all an act, like Houdini, a sleight of hand. Just like the hills that converge and rise, roll and fall, and creep around at night like cups in a guessing game. In the morning you swear that one of the hills used to be over there, not here.

The cows grow older. Their faces change to look like regular old cow-faces from any children's book. The hawks stop fooling around and return to pouncing on mice in the fields. Stars multiply. The sheep count them to get to sleep.

Expectations

When the phone rang Sarah waited for her machine to click on, and when she heard Walt's voice sliding through its tiny speaker she picked up the receiver. Simple. It seemed so simple to change a life. She said hello. Then her legs felt like crooked stilts, so she eased into a wobbly kitchen chair.

Walt's "I love you's" came easily, came quickly, always before she could hang up the phone. For Sarah, a long, complicated maze fitted the words to the feelings. Today Sarah said what she always said when she ran down that blocked, tangled path at the end of a conversation. She said, "I know you do, Walter. I know."

Silence. Had Sarah hung up first? Had Walter? Had days passed? Sarah glanced out the kitchen window. Tree branches shimmered in the late afternoon, the sun peeking out for a brief presentation. She could hear the neighborhood girls singing. School was out. The sun shifted across the dusty linoleum in long lush rays. She had to take a shower and pull herself together for her date later that evening. A date? Seriously. Who did she think she was?

Sarah adjusted the shower faucets. Hot was cold and cold was hot. Sarah could never remember. She stepped in. Giddy first-date jitters made her feel cold in the warming water. She tried to anticipate all of the unrealized contradictions and incompatibilities that would lurk under the surface. She had already assured herself she wouldn't sleep with Scott. She just needed a little boost, something to help her self-esteem. No harm in flirting if it helped her get some perspective, right?

Sarah had met Scott at the coffee shop down the street where she'd taken a part-time job after her separation from Walt. Hunched into the corner by the far wall, he typed on his laptop with an earnest, endearing concentration. Soon he showed up on Sarah's daily lists—the litanies she made these days in order to keep her sanity. At first Scott was simply clothing: green shirt, faded Levis, Hush Puppies. Then as she noticed him noticing her, the lists focused on his face: curved nose, blue eyes, dimples. Finally, she recorded bits of conversation: "Totally cool to sleep in the middle of the day." "I love double features in empty movie theaters." "The macchiato. Perfection in a tiny cup."

Soon, seeing Scott was the highlight of Sarah's week. She walked home to dust and complications, lists without a thing crossed off, and the blinking red light on her answering machine. Her options seemed strangely scripted. She could press the button, start a new list, go to sleep, make some rice, pet the cat. The life in her apartment could not compare to the thrill of a crush on an anonymous man in a coffee shop.

Sarah wondered why she'd ever married. Trying to understand another person in the scope of until-death-do-us-part only
solved for failure. It seemed simple enough in theory, of course—but
then her head became bogged down and baffled by Walt—by her
reactions to him, by their inability to treat each other fairly even
though they'd promised to do just that while standing in expensive
clothes in front of a lot of people. She knew Walt was her true love,
her first real love. But she also knew in some way loving him had
nothing to do with the life she led with him.

The phone rang again as she turned off the cold and
hot. Sarah lunged to get to it before the machine clicked on. She
assumed it was Scott. She knew her hello held a kind of subdued,
but gleeful anticipation. Instead, the voice of her father-in-law, Big
Walt, boomed at her through the receiver. Sarah slid to the floor. She
let her wet back scrape along the shag carpet. When she stood up
minutes later, she could see her outline smashed into the brown
spiky mess.

Big Walt made most of his calls from the highway on his cell
phone. His voice filtered in and out of reception. "Sarah ... to hear
your voice ... so long since ... flying in tomorrow ... like to go to lunch."

Sarah didn't know what Big Walt did or didn't know about
her and Walt. She yelled back into the static. "Um. I don't know."

The static receded and Big Walt came through loud and
clear, yelling back at her. He said, "Well, I'm on my way to the air-
port right now. It's a layover until six p.m. in Pittsburgh. Let's meet
for lunch. One o'clock would be good for you, right Sarah?"

"Yes, of course. Okay, Dad."

"And Walter's busy I take it. It'll just be you and me then?"
The static returned, blurring his last two words.

Sarah yelled, "Where?"

"That Cushion place ... long time since ... better make it one thirty... Good talking ...." Then the line went dead.

"Tunnel," Sarah mumbled. She waited for Big Walt to call back, but the phone remained silent. She looked at her outline on the floor. "I look fat," Sarah said to her cat as he walked through the impression, turned, and curled to sleep where Sarah's shoulders had just been. She had lunch plans with Big Walt, her father-in-law. Sarah made quotation mark signs with both hands. She said, "Separated."

Her apartment's buzzer rang. "Fuck," Sarah said. She grabbed her bra and underwear. She pressed the intercom button.

Scott said, "Hello there."

Sarah said, "C'mon up." She pushed the blue button to let him in and rushed to get dressed. As she zipped her jeans, she could hear Scott's clomps up the stairs, then came his quick rapping knock on the door as she pulled her T-shirt down over her still-wet hair.

Seeing Scott standing in her apartment in the same clothes he wore to the coffee shop, having him enter this other part of her life, did not help.

Scott looked around at her unpacked boxes. "Nice decor. Very Hooverville," he said. Scott sat down on the floor crossed-legged and grinned. His bangs fell into his eyes, and a part of Sarah wanted to gently brush them away. Another part of her said, "You're going to have cat hair all over you. I can't keep up no matter how much I vacuum." She stepped into socks and shoes, pulled her wet hair up into a ponytail, stacked a pile of toppled books, placed a few scattered lists into a dresser drawer.

Scott awkwardly hugged the cat and pet its head too hard. He said, "So."

Sarah said, "So."

Scott stood up. "We'll just make the 7:15 showing if we hurry."

"Cool," said Sarah.

"Cool," said Scott.

A chill spread over Sarah's body. It sunk down into her veins. All signals said stay home, make some tea. But she stepped forward and out the door, locking it behind her, checking to make sure the lock stayed tight. She reopened the door to make sure she'd turned on the kitchen light, then she checked the coffee maker. It was off. Scott laughed nervously before he followed her down the stairs.

After the movie and over beers, nothing changed. Sarah heard herself forcing one word replies like, "Cool." She told Scott the same stories that she'd told so many times she'd started embellishing them to keep them fresh. She talked about Nebraska, and he talked about Michigan. She talked about Vermont, and he talked about DC. They talked about Pittsburgh—argued about whether it would turn around or plunge back into economic uncertainty. Scott bought two rounds; Sarah bought one. The jukebox played Neil Young and then Nirvana. Sarah yawned, and seeing her, Scott yawned. They both laughed and Sarah said, "Well? I'll call it a night, I guess."

Scott pulled up in front of her building. Her cat's silhouette waited in the kitchen window. Scott said, "I like your cat."

Sarah said, "Is that the first line of a dirty joke?"

Scott turned to her and stuck out his hand. Sarah shook it.

Scott said, "I'll see you around." He smiled.

Sarah smiled back, "Me too."

Scott drove away as she unlocked her door. Her apartment looked unfamiliar and empty. Her kitchen table, her cat, her futon haphazardly made in the other room. Boxes. Thinking of Scott's smile, Sarah debated if it offered pity, condescension, or empathy.

She walked to the table. The cat sat in the opposite chair as if ready to have a serious discussion. Sarah said, "A handshake. What does that mean?" The cat yawned and then continued to stare in his blank, expectant way.

It certainly wasn't the excitement and fireworks Sarah had remembered first dates to be. It seemed mechanical: a movie, a beer, a walk to the car, a good night. Sarah started to list these things on the back of a credit card offer. Everything about the date made her miss what had been the comfortableness of Walt. He knew where she liked to sit in the movie theater. He didn't try to talk to her after the movie had started, and he didn't psychoanalyze every character when it finished. He was just Walt, the person her body responded to, the person whose hair she played with while he drove the car, the person who laid his hand on her knee during the scary scenes, the person who asked the concessions worker to layer the butter over the popcorn as the bucket filled so it would be properly dispersed.

But then the happy memories gave way to the Walt she had loathed that last month before she moved out. Walt staring at her with disgust when she came into the room. Walt walking out the door before she had time to finish the story she was telling him. Walt slowly putting his magazine down, slowly setting his drink down, slowly looking up at her, slowly and methodically asking, "What Sarah? What is it you want?" His face glowing yellow in the dim halo of the reading chair light.

The sun rose with the cat twitching its tail, with Sarah staring out into the street, with the upstairs neighbors shuffling to sleep, then out of it. The sun rose, and Sarah stood up to make coffee.

Sarah and Walt had never been able to afford Cushion on their own. They always waited until Big Walt visited. It was the only place he ever wanted to go anyway. And here she was. On her own this time.

She found a pair of blue linen pants that had managed to stay unwrinkled in the move. The only thing she found to match them was a white V-neck T-shirt. She didn't know if Big Walt would approve of such casual dress. She put on a necklace and some lipstick, and by the time she buckled herself into the car and checked herself in the rearview mirror, she decided she could pass the fashion muster.

When she walked into the restaurant, though, all the nerves she'd managed to conceal cracked. The forced smile from the host seemed to say, "Dear lord, you look like hell." Sarah took a deep breath. Held it. Big Walt welcomed her with his arms spread wide. He hugged her and said she looked beautiful, said he was privileged to have lunch with such a flower. Sarah pat his back. She blushed. She didn't cry until they were seated.

Not little tears that could easily be excused, oh no, she burst out into big ugly sobs. Her face contorted, and she had to reluctantly use the linen napkin to blow her nose, twice. People from other tables cautiously gawked. Big Walt moved his chair over beside hers. Raised a finger for the waiter. As always, one magically appeared. "Scotch," he said. "Scotch, right Sarah? That's what we need. Water. Oh, we have that. Two doubles. Straight up. Straight away."

Sarah inhaled unevenly. "Thanks, Dad. Sorry."

"Right. So then. Thank you, sir." The waiter set down the two thick tumblers. Big Walt raised his. Handed Sarah hers and said, "To strong times."

After another scotch they ordered lunch. Already drunk, Sarah ordered a seared tuna salad with fresh organic greens. Big Walt ordered young baby goat. The bread came and Sarah tore into it to try to catch up with herself before she said something excruciatingly stupid.

Big Walt occupied himself with his butter knife and his bread, spreading crumbs in a shower around his small salad plate. He raised his empty glass toward the bar, and the waiter migrated over. Sarah thought that they had to see Big Walt coming with more than an ounce of trepidation. "Another, Sarah?"

"Sure," she said. Big Walt's preoccupation with detail calmed her. Not asking a thing of her was a good strategy to keep her from crying again.

The food came. Big Walt looked at his watch. "So, what's this that's going on with you and Walt? This separation that he talks about like it's a mystery. Whose idea was it? Yours? His? Mine?" He laughed. "Surely, I didn't have anything to do with this one, did I?"

"No, Walt, I hate to disappoint you, but this one has nothing to do with you at all." And Big Walt did look a little disappointed. "No. I guess it was my idea. But sort of mutual. I think I'm suffering more than Walt, if that means anything."

"Yes, it means something. Everything always means something."

Sarah tried to talk about Walt, about the problems, but the conversation always circled back to her. Sarah talked about her past, about her ex-lovers and her inability to forgive, to go forward without forgetting the past. She talked about her own fears, that she could never be a kind or generous person because she had been wounded along the way. She talked about her awful, boring date the night before with Scott.

Soon the waiter came offering desserts and then coffee. Big Walt nodded and told her to keep going. His fork remained suspended above his key lime tart. His coffee slowly cooled.

"You see, Dad, I expected things to be different this time. I thought everything would be easy for Walt and me because we were in love. But the problem is me. I have too many problems for one man, I guess. I mean, there are no other men, but you get what I mean, right?" Sarah took a big gulp from her water glass and pushed a strand of hair behind her ear. "There's been so much confusion, and I just keep going forward instead of insisting on resolution. I feel like I have to look back now and resolve every relationship I've ever had before I can start becoming a decent person to Walt. Jesus."

Sarah had no idea where all these words came from. She wanted to shove them back into her mouth, to wash them away with another scotch. She hadn't ever put her life together in the way she presented it to Big Walt. She thought maybe the mundane conversation with Scott the night before had nudged her into saying something, anything, of substance.

"But it's not just me," Sarah continued. "It's him, too. He won't admit he's bored. It's both of us together. It's too complex, and no one seems to understand."

Big Walt looked at his plate. He seemed surprised to see his dessert untouched. He finished it in four swift bites. He downed his coffee in three swallows. He raised his hand for the check. Sarah felt foolish. She fidgeted with her napkin. She said, "Well, I imagine that you need to get going. Does your flight leave soon?"

Big Walt looked at her through his sleepy drunkard's eyes. He touched her arm. "Let's go to the bar. Let's just go over here and sit for a while."

"I'm sure it will all work out one way or another, Walt," Sarah said. "I'm sorry to involve you at all. It's my black hole. I'll crawl my way out of it or get spit out the other side."

Unable to stop the lunch drunk they'd worked themselves into, they both ordered beer. Two Stella Artois sat side by side sweating onto cardboard coasters. Big Walt looked at his label, addressing it instead of Sarah. "My wife. Eloise. You've met her, right? My ex-wife, that is. You've met her?"

"Yes, we've gone to visit her in California. And then at the wedding. She's very sweet."

"Yes, she's very, very sweet. Me, on the other hand, I am not a sweet person." Sarah protested, and Big Walt interrupted, "No. You don't know."

Sarah watched the bartender dry three wine glasses, hold the third up to the light and wipe it again before hanging it above the bar.

"When Eloise and I had Walt we'd already been married for what seemed to me then like a long time. We were married in our twenties, and then she had Walt when she was thirty. That was late back then, and you know we were set in our ways already. We had dinner parties and cocktail parties and golf and card games and suddenly there was, well, Walt." Big Walt turned to look at Sarah.

"But I learned to change. Once he was old enough to golf and boat and swim at the club, everything got easier. Eloise lived for

Walt, and I know they're still very close. I know she wanted to have a whole big family, like the one she came from. I said one. I ranted and raved and threatened to leave her if she ever found herself pregnant again. Then I went out and got, well I made sure it wouldn't happen. And she cried a lot then. I'd find her crying in the kitchen, or I'd hear her late at night when she thought I was asleep. I made her suffer in ways I'll never understand."

Walter's words slurred now as he blinked his watery eyes. "So when Walter graduated from high school," he said, "I felt I had done my duty. I was done. That's when Eloise bought the puppy. I came home and there was this little brown yappy thing running in circles in the kitchen. She said she couldn't help herself. She was grinning like a schoolgirl. I know she was happy that day." He looked at the bartender and mouthed water. "Do you want another, Sarah? No, we're fine. Thanks."

Sarah asked, "So what happened?"

"I left. I said forget it."

"Really?"

"I took my best bottle of scotch, my golf clubs, and a suitcase of clothes. I stayed in a hotel down the street for two months."

"Did she get rid of the dog?"

"Hmm. I can't even remember now. It doesn't really matter, does it? It was over right then and there. I came back for a few years, but it was over. So much time had passed, and neither of us had anything close to what we wanted."

"Years?"

"You know what's worse? I miss her every day. I miss what I wanted us to be."

Big Walt looked at his watch again, and then stood up.

"Shall we? I have to head out. It was so very good seeing you, Sarah." She followed behind, swaying slightly from the alcohol and the dull sun as it hit them on the street.

"There's the taxi." He hugged Sarah. "You'll be fine. We're all fine, really. It's just expectations, that's all."

And he was gone, and Sarah was alone staring at the antique store across the street. A brown dog sat by the front doors waiting on its owner, its tongue hanging loose. It cocked its head quizzically at Sarah as her fuzzy reflection bounced back from the store's plate-glass front, cars zipping by intermittently, blocking her view.

Digging

I dug deeper as the crusty earth folded itself up and away. Digging for potatoes at a time when I should have had something better to do—a man to feed. Something.

I stuck my naked feet into the dirt, wiggled my toes, stretched my stiff back, bringing my arms straight up to the sky. I could feel the potatoes—cancerous lumps I needed to surgeon out.

My Italian mother hated the Irish, the potato, the boats that had brought my father's family into port. She hated "the whole drunken lot" as she called them—what with all of the dancing and whiskey—a culture that had produced her husband, a man who could woo her into a barn at fifteen, knock her up, and live by his mistake happy as a clam until the day he died.

After Joe had left me for good, I chopped down the tomato plants. I'd been the good Italian girl, waited to marry the decent guy, had rows of immaculate canning: stewed tomatoes, tomato sauce, hot peppers, and sweet relish on the cellar shelves. Broken hearts, glistening—jar after jar.

For the women in my family, it's a genetic trait to seek unhappiness, groom discomfort, take misery and rock it gently to sleep night after night.

My father died. Joe left.

I put the potatoes in a bowl, in a place where the morning light washes over them—rinsed and scrubbed squeaky clean. In the morning, when I stumble from bedroom to bathroom to kitchen, they look alive and miraculous: a beacon.

The Bottle

Francine cracked the bottle on the table edge. She smashed it twice. It was a thick wine bottle and it blossomed open with ragged edges. Afterward she set the bottle upright on the tabletop, its fractured top like a crown. The table's slippery wooden surface smelled of lemon oil and perfectly reflected the bottle in reverse.

The candles sputtered, and little pins of light bounced back off the green glass. Francine's eyebrows tilted toward the bridge of her nose—sloped in to say she was thinking hard. Seth watched her eyes, the thoughts ticking through; he considered the possibilities from here on in. Everything changes when someone smashes a wine bottle without preamble or warning.

"Have a bad day, Franci?" Seth finally asked, leaning back in his chair. The chair's two back legs ground some loose glass into the wooden floorboards. "The accountants at your back again?" He twisted his napkin from his lap, laid it out on the table like a broken bird.

They'd been having a fine dinner. Seth had come home early to get things going. He'd rinsed the brussels sprouts—fresh and in season—then let them soak in salted water until they sparkled green. He chopped up garlic and sautéed it until it was crispy. He cooked some pancetta and pasta, pulled a bottle of red from the rack, and splashed the wine into big goblet glasses.

Now the empty bottle balanced on the table like a dare.

Francine eyed the fractured bottle. She felt better, for sure. But now she'd have to explain herself. She hated words. They did her in every time. What she wanted was action. Action without repercussion or discussion. Pure, clean *decision making*. But she knew this wasn't how the world worked—or it wasn't how Seth's world worked. Things were talked through and hashed and re-hashed and reasoned. She wanted some unreasonableness every now and then. Was that asking too much?

Francine finished the last little splash of wine in her glass. She carefully carried her plate to the sink, held it above the slick gray metal, and then let it drop with a crack. God that felt good. But now she'd have to explain that, too. Seth eyed her up.

This was new territory in their ten-year marriage.

Everything was changing all around Francine. She couldn't seem to stop it. She liked repression and denial and passive-aggression. It seemed so much easier. She liked quick meals with frozen vegetables. She wanted to swim upstream, away from all these foodies and do-gooders.

"Franci. Why don't you just head out of the kitchen before you break something I really care about?" Seth said. He held tightly to his wine glass, a favorite from a set he'd carted back from Italy years before. Seth loved things. He looked hurt and worn out. He just wasn't up for her, was he? He thought he could do it, could take her on, but Francine could see the fabric of their relationship wearing thin.

She stomped out of the kitchen. The loose floorboards made the table shake, clanging the glasses and cutlery and serving dish together in a food symphony. She strode into the living room and out the front door.

The bottle had snapped so easily. Like a chicken's neck. Not clean, but easy. She'd have to explain, but not now. She inhaled the clean, sharp country air. Fall at hand and the world seemed reset, beautiful and crisp and new. The moon wavered back at her through the creepy tree limbs, as if it understood and needed no explanation.

The world just didn't fit right. Francine thought she might say that to Seth. Tell him how the world wasn't fitting right. Try to show him what didn't work. Like their beautiful house she didn't deserve. And him. She probably didn't deserve him either. The world was so big and the hours so long. How could she have predicted this ending? She exhaled. Crossed her arms.

The bottle broke so neatly. It cracked and drew Seth's eyes up to hers from his meal. He saw her clearly then, she was sure— his fork suspended above his dwindling plate of pasta. What she won't tell him is that he looked at her then like the first time he'd laid eyes on her. And that made it worth it.

It made her want to do it again.

Transplanting

T he narrow path curved to the right through the trees. October, and its branches heaved color at the skyline. Betty, our dog, sauntered along beside us, dragging her leash like a sash for a pageant. We carried plastic water bottles and wrapped wool scarves around our necks over long-sleeved shirts. The park's paths corkscrewed around themselves up to Parker Hill, where we could see all of Boston.

Dogs bounded on the top of the hill like a crazy after-party, a little Yorkie named Daisy holding her own. We surmised the circling hawk could easily lift her and her cute red harness off to oblivion. But Daisy sniffed and romped, lifted one of her tiny legs to pee.

We'd recently transplanted Betty from Kansas. She'd been on the open Plains one minute, and then in a two-bedroom apartment the next. You wonder how dogs process these things. But she was a good sport and looked popular with this new East Coast dog crowd. Sophisticated. Ready to take on both the urban howlers and little lap yappers.

Tim and I had met in Boston and then moved to the middle of the country. We'd both lived in other cities, had other lives before this one came together. Older now, it was hard to faze us.

We looked across to the city. The leaves red, orange, and yellow in the fancy foreground. The sky clear blue; the city sparkling. Hard to imagine winter or rain. Only this fall day. Forever.

We hadn't loved Kansas, but leaving it had made for some trouble, simply because we'd tried so hard to make it work. The loneliness, the twang. We wanted to dig in. But when Tim got the big job offer, we jumped, embracing the idea of reverse pioneering back to the East Coast.

Later that day we drove to the ocean. Piles of mossy seaweed, the rank, salty smell. It all whispered: this is where you belong—the wind rushing from the water, the waves lapping as a thin line of birds scampered to-and-fro.

And we breathed together, side by side, Tim and me. We felt each other taking it in, exhaling it back out.

But after we left the shore, got in our car, packed in the big dog, toweled her off, wiped her slobber, in that close space, we couldn't say a thing. Slumped in our seats, we were terribly, suddenly sad, again.

I pulled over. I tapped the steering wheel. "No surprises, right? We knew we'd be happy here, again. We knew that."

Tim stared out the window, rolled down the window so he could hear the gulls and taste the salty air. "But you," he said.

I waited for him to finish, but he didn't. We sat there breathing. Betty the dog snored softly in the back. She was old, after all, and couldn't go all day like she used to. I realized then that she would die soon. I waited a bit, and then turned the key, pulled slowly back into the lane that led us away and out to the interstate and back to the city that was our city now, and out to dinner with newly found friends with small talk and candlelight. And then finally to the apartment where the floorboards creaked as we readied for bed. I wondered if the downstairs neighbors tracked our days by the sound of our footsteps above them.

Of course we had chatted through dinner, but it was the kind of performance you put on for others, those on the outside who can't know what's going on inside a couple, inside the car, the apartment. Our heads. The retelling of stories we'd heard each other tell a hundred times before.

Our apartment felt permanently chilled with the fall air settling in, the sun sunk and night prying its fingers into everything. We piled on a couple of quilts, climbed in. Betty splayed out by the foot of the bed. The cat clawed at a door, played with a squeaky toy in the living room, and then stopped.

I said, "But?"

Tim rolled my way. The bed heaved a little and then sagged. He touched my shoulder. We'd had the bed for years. An antique store purchase, the metal frame so beautiful in our house on the Plains, now here looking like an awkward transplant. "But," he said, "you can't go back." His voice came out soft. "It never works."

We already felt the city binding us in its grip, getting smaller each day. Tightening, shrinking, until we couldn't possibly fit inside it anymore. Until we ran in tighter and tighter circles while the hawks circled and dove.

Back Porch

We're sitting on my crooked back porch. We're screened in and drinking a bottle of wine. It would look simple and romantic if I didn't know how much we'd already had to drink. Instead, it's a crazy, lusty blur. This first night together.

We're drinking wine and there's a candle lit. It quivers and swings in the late, dark night. Bugs are making whirring noises and we've only just met a week or two before—you awkwardly asking to sit at my table, me saying, "Fine," and then continuing to read.

But right now, I would stay out with you all night. I would stay on this back porch forever.

And what I'll remember is you, sitting on the crooked steps beside my crooked back porch chair. You leaning toward me and asking, "Can I kiss you?"

And me, looking at you and silently thinking, Can I do this all again?

And you saying, "I've been staring at your lips for weeks."

And me not believing you but loving you for saying it anyway.

And then.

We kissed.

Pittsburgh Women

I n Pittsburgh, women carry large baskets of coins. They scatter the nickels, dimes, and quarters up and down the city streets, as if they're sowing corn or oats or wildflower seeds. When they've finished, the women stoop and twist to gather the change back up again.

When they're done for the day, the women go home to make dinner for their families. They press moist dough with their firm fingers. They sit at tables with cooling cups of coffee. The sunlight fades from first one hilly horizon, then the next. The Pittsburgh women rub lotion over each finger and up to the elbow on each muscular arm. The lotion smells like roses and cinnamon and midnight rain.

When it's dark, the women walk outside. They hear the clank of machines, the rattle of trains, the breeze tapping its way through every single tree. The women inhale with their hands on their hips; they strike wooden matches to hold the flame to the fuses of fireworks, which pop and sizzle as they dart up into the night.

After the colors have drained, sooty ashes tumble from the sky. The women carefully sweep them into piles, bending quickly to read fortunes, predicting long lives filled with hope and lust and passion. At night, they sleep soundly in big beds, coins shifting gently with each breath.

Birds in Relation to Other Things

Birds circle noiselessly near my window these days. They're black dots. Larger, then smaller. There are times when I open my window and they hop cautiously inside, escaping the soot and perpetual fog of our town.

I remain in this small room. Here, it's always dusty twilight. One window pane is loose and cracked. It rattles with the breeze. You are very far away.

I talk softly into a coal-black phone after it has rung twice. I listen to my voice. Reassuring. Reassuring. I put down the receiver.

You've gotten into an old car, a car in which you're comfortable. You glance in the rearview mirror and drink juice from a bottle.

The birds have come to know me well. They trust me. They perch on my lamp, chair, and ashtray. They are small and move quietly around my soiled clothes and hair, my dirty fingernails. I do not want to touch them. I think they realize this.

Sometimes the birds raise important questions. Ones I cannot answer. They peck at my thin carpet like chickens. But they aren't. They're birds with homes just as small as mine.

I know if I was just kind enough I would be able to hear you coming. I would know your car's headlights and run toward you with my arms raised.

It's late, and the birds have gone. I listen to street sounds.

If I was kind enough, I would be able to care about one thing. I would understand what the birds are getting at. I would be able to understand what it's like beyond myself and the things I own.

I would spare a crust of bread.

This Is What I Want

I'm sitting at my window again. This time it's day. Clear. Bright. Not like the days of fog and soot I've told you about. Not like the scariness that comes with deep, black night. I'm waiting patiently for a sign to come from the sky, up from the ground, out of my cold cup of tea. I'm waiting patiently—but that never lasts.

It turns to dusk—things smell musty. The cats start scuttling, and then where am I? Here without you and your insights. Here where the timid knock at the door means no real thing, means no real person has come to call when I open it, means this is just an old house that has things to say I cannot hear, cannot understand—or refuse to.

I do not want to talk to houses or cats or the birds scratching at the top of my chimney. I want to talk to you softly—shift, so my blouse shifts, so you can catch just a glimpse of the blue lace on my new bra, of my soft white skin. I want you to be sure of yourself, sure that what you want is me—or the birds or cats. Something.

I sigh now. It's not for effect. It's lonely in this city—its sky bleeding red and orange into gray muck, then blank black. It's sad trying to see outlines and only glimpsing my own bending reflection with old eyes that tell so much more than I want them to.

I pull the blinds.

I turn my back to the wall, and I turn slowly in my hand the empty salt shaker I've been meaning to fill. It's strong and solid and doesn't break as I toss it against the marble of the fireplace.

Even when I try again.

It's a still life—the coal-black phone. The orange arm chair. The green sweater, black cat. We all sit very quietly waiting for the signal that means it's okay. It's all okay. This life of yours—good choice, keep going.

Everything Here

He has been here for days now, and these days seem like minutes to her. She fiddles with her bra strap—checks the pie in the oven. The old metal door creaks once quickly with the opening, then with the closing. The gas jets kick on underneath with a slow hiss.

She sits down at the table with a cup of coffee. Steam rising. She knows what she wants is the future here and now. She wants to be able to look back on years and years of happiness and think of this life of hers as one big day.

For now, she stirs the soup. It simmers and bubbles on the back burner. The smells trickle down the hallway toward the bedroom and slide quietly out the back window.

She sets the table, checks her watch. She hears the creak of his first step up the staircase. She grins.

III

What It Would Look Like

I'm sitting in the theater—dusty old seats, the smell of soggy popcorn, sticky soda, and cheap chocolate. The dust that has risen glitters and turns in the sputtering projector light. The projector hums patiently from up in the control booth. Box fans sit in the aisles. An air conditioner spits and rattles in the lobby. Only a few lonely patrons sit in the musty theater, but I'm sure others will show.

I'm here to watch me and you live our lives like movie stars.

Suddenly, there I am on the lime-green couch. We're in Technicolor, and you're coming down the stairs. Jack, the dog, runs scampering ahead of you. You have glasses on that make you look smart, and a white shirt that makes you look rich. Your pants are blue; your shoes black and shiny. You look at me and smile. I look at you and smile, and immediately we remind the audience of Spencer Tracy and Katherine Hepburn in *Adam's Rib*—except I don't have the jawline, and you have the wrong build. Things are light, but serious. We're happy; you can tell by the sparkle in our eyes. I tell you a story about the dead pigeon I saw my neighbor carrying around my yard by one fragile wing tip. I tell you what he was yelling, which was: "Andre! You son of a bitch, look! I think it's dead. Andre!"

I tell you I don't know if Andre is the man's son or dog.

You laugh and say, "God. It's so great, these stories you tell." You're sitting on the edge of an oddly shaped orange chair, leaning in my direction with your forearms resting on your thighs. You've given me your complete attention.

My story is dramatic, and I'm waving my arms as I tell you about the glass of scotch my neighbor carries in his other hand. About the BB gun he picks up later and aims at a squirrel and instead hits my window. I wear a 1940s cream-colored suit fitted to reveal my ample bust with just a little cleavage, my slim waist. I wear thick black heels. And now the music begins, and we slide into a choreographed dance. I notice my skirt is slit to make my movements easier—your pants seem to be made of a stretchy material that hugs your thighs with each tight turn. We smile and take big steps that lead us through the living room into the brightly lit kitchen. We miraculously continue to sing and dance while we chop vegetables, brown onions, clean and sauté the shrimp.

We're absolutely charming—and fit.

The music ends, and the few people in the theater shift in their seats. They shake their popcorn containers like awkward maracas to get at the bigger popped kernels. We're all anxious to see what comes next.

As the sun moves behind the clouds, weak shafts of light filter through the slats of the blinds, sweep across us, and glide into the kitchen as the movie fades to black and white. A heated dialogue begins almost immediately, and we aren't even out of breath from the dancing.

My face is half-concealed in shadow.

I say, "So. This is what you call dinner?"

You turn quickly and say, "Dinner. Lunch. What do you want from me?"

I say, "I call them how I see them. You're out of focus, as usual."

I sharpen a knife. Soon you slam a drawer and are driving a meat cleaver hard into the cutting board to make a point.

We're cool. I throw my shoulders back—you set your feet firmly apart. You're pointing the knife in my direction. In the audience, I'm suspecting one of us might die. This is how cool we are.

I say, "Dinner is only as good as the person making it." Then I tilt my head and swing my hair slowly over my shoulder. I say, "So. How good are you?"

You say, "I guess you'll see when the time comes."

I say, "I guess we'll see," and walk back into the living room holding a ticking timer in my hands, moving my hips. I look once over my shoulder and raise my eyebrows. Then as you stand alone in the kitchen looking after me, I twist the dial to make it ring.

This is the movie I'm watching. It's us, and I know just before the words THE END bleed onto the screen, we will have kissed. I'll push you away slightly, then pull you back, then we'll kiss again. And at this point it will be clear to everyone sitting around me, including the drunk guy who came in late—even to the stale popcorn shoved down into the seats and the swirling dust—that we're in love and we will live happily ever after in this second-run theater.

But this is only the movie. In real life, we've missed all our cues. In real life, you come running down the stairs, too loud—you have on sweatpants with your white shirt. Jack barks upstairs at some stray leaves he sees through the window. It's a foggy, rainy day, but you're smiling. I'm wearing baggy jeans and a wrinkled shirt. My hair is a mess because I'm almost asleep on the faded green couch, and cranky because I've been waiting too long for you to get ready. I yawn and smile back. You rush me because we will be late for the movie we're going to see. You pull me up from the couch, but we miss the dance sequence because we decide that instead of cooking we'll get food from Thai Blossom on West Hickory Street on the way to the theater.

The vegetables sit untouched and rot quietly in your dark refrigerator. The sun shifts, and slanting light crosses an empty kitchen.

On the way to the car, I tell you about my neighbor and the dead pigeon, about the scotch, and the small flower of a crack in my window, but the sound guy can't possibly pick this up. In this life that isn't a movie, we are never able to reach a point of synchronicity. We never see the credits coming, so we never kiss. Love never begins.

And you would say, if I told you this, that the movie never shows what happens after the credits roll. The hot August night when I walk in on you and Emily. The sad awkward tangle of bodies struggling on the sagging couch. The sweat. My one short scream like a starter's pistol. Jack running and whimpering under the table as the neighbors' lights turn on, then off, like reluctant lightning bugs down the street. And no eloquent explanations, just both of us tired and sorry and so fed up.

We fade apart, never to see each other again except in the

random grocery aisle where we wave by lifting a few fingers from the rail of the cart, or in the bookstore, shuffling our feet against the nubby carpet, reluctantly tipping covers to show each other titles.

We get to the movie barely on time. Pull carefully packaged Thai Blossom from where we've hidden it in our jackets as we run giggling to our seats—middle center. We've learned not to share. It's too complicated. We've learned to leave our knees untouching, to watch the movie closely so we can talk about it for hours later, to whisper, "This is so damn good," quietly in each other's ears. We nod silently at the good lines and see where the acting is weak. Our seats creak as we shift our bodies, as we get more comfortable and the tension rises. We've learned to wipe our mouths as we carefully pucker our lips to napkins. We've learned to relax until the credits roll.

Las Vegas Women

I n Las Vegas, women are made of polyester and plastic. They appear very authentic, fooling even the closest observer.

They do not think souvenir dog brushes or big bright neon elephants or all-you-can-eat four a.m. hot dog stands are funny. If you crack a joke in front of one of them, they pause as if they hear a rainstorm coming, then continue brewing coffee or counting postcards into stacks of twenty.

Once when I asked where the bathroom was, I saw a Las Vegas woman smile. It was like the Mona Lisa. She smiled as if all women in Las Vegas were born knowing instinctively where all bathrooms were and that I was without a doubt not one of them.

Down the hall and to the left.

In Las Vegas, women wear bright colors and lots of glittery gold to convince others they are not surrounded by sage brush and prairie-dog towns. It is in this way they resemble small lizards.

Women in Las Vegas have sex in rooms where the cast of neon lights blinks randomly on and off in blue, green, and red. They do it very, very slowly. Due to this pacing, their makeup stays intact and they are able to look alert far longer than women from out of town.

Garden Inside

1. FLOWER BED

Once your mother let you plant your own little garden in her yard. Your dad dug up an oval patch over by the carport with the rototiller. When you went to the nursery to pick your flowers, you chose the tiny purple thing and the fuzzy blue things that looked like folded carpets. You bought marigolds. Because you were a confused and absentminded child, you didn't understand that plants came from seeds and bulbs.

It seemed anticlimactic, putting the little plants into the little bed. They looked very much the same: Before. After. You had thought they would change—grow, morph into something exquisite and indescribable.

You were a serious child, critical of your garden, because you understood that somewhere there was a place where lush, chaotic flowers flowed out of their beds onto sidewalks. You understood that beyond the shrubs and flagpoles and geometric squares of grass, there was a kind of humility and awe you couldn't feel standing there looking at your crisp, perky flowers. You stood in the gravel driveway with a tiny shovel in your hand, staring, waiting for directions.

2. THE LAST GOOD DAY IN THE FIRST GARDEN

There are moments of pure joy in this world. The trick is how to find them. And suddenly, a miracle. The neighbors are quiet. They aren't yelling at their dog or calling their kid a dog or beating on each other. It's peaceful. Silent.

Inhale. One. Two. Three.

The late afternoon light hits the drying cornstalks, and you gasp. You wonder if there's a way you could capture that color, move it to your living room walls. Will you ever be able to tear yourself away from this garden, leave this house and these neighbors? It's getting harder to sleep, and if you call the police, they will know you've called the police and will bang on your door accusing you of calling the police. So. But still.

You will remember the kind of love this garden induced in you for the rest of your life. When you leave, it will feel as if you've abandoned a child. That first spring, when you see daffodils poking up in other people's yards, you'll cry.

You sigh.

It's hard to believe that corn can grow so fast in June and July. Some days you see your life pass before your eyes. Others, you sit and listen to time passing you by. It's a miracle. And then, just as suddenly, the stalks die standing straight up.

Peace. Quiet.

Then a rustling, as hollow cornstalks nestle into each other. The light in the yard is shimmering dull orange. You turn to face it. You won't worry about the big things right now. You won't worry about the small things. You won't think about loss or how your future is looming and vacant. Even as you hear a small cry come from the house next door, even as the muffled noises begin out of their open kitchen window.

You steal this moment. You take it away.

3. NEW HOUSE

It took a long time to find the new house with the long, skinny, sloping yard. The real estate woman nodded at your husband, and then you, and declared the yard had potential.

Your husband assures you the new garden will be better than the old one. This feels like a betrayal. You know nothing will ever touch the perfection of that garden: tomato plants crammed in near the rose bush and fennel, basil and columbine in the corner with strawberry plants and lettuce. The small crop of first wheat, then sorghum, then flax. The rhubarb, the wildflowers, the corn and sunflowers—everything crazy and brilliant, coexisting beyond all the skeptics.

And the new yard: it's grass. Even though all your nice, new, quiet neighbors assure you that the old woman you bought the house from once had a huge garden. All you see is grass with one scraggily oak tree to the side.

It's exhausting thinking about turning it into something

else. You stare at the slope of the yard, at the neighbor's dog. Dude barks at you every time you shove the manual push mower by him.

As soon as it turns warm, you drag a metal lawn chair under the tree with all its missing limbs and cracked bark. Now you huddle there in its shade. You're unsure if you're looking to get or give comfort.

The leaves above you quake in the breeze as your husband jabs the shovel deep into the ground and wedges free a patch of lawn. He turns it over in one swift movement and, earth up, puts it back down, burying the grass with a few more quick, short pokes. He steps to the side. Begins again.

4. THE GARDEN: LATE AUGUST

The tomatoes have wiggled their way up the stakes, corseted here and there with stretches of last year's tights. They've put on gaudy red and yellow earrings in order to impress the neighbors. The kale has matching ruffled slips, and the lone brussels sprout, a gift from Christina, sings an operetta beside throngs of adoring corn. And you are left to wonder why the swiss chard seems to have an inferiority complex, while the gourds have befriended the beans in a mildly erotic orgy that flows down the yard and over the retaining wall. The tree is prudish and dismissive, and you have become an innocent bystander. The garden revolution is in full swing, leaving behind all good intentions, leaving behind the master plan.

Alive, Almost

J ackie crumpled up the letter in her fist. She found the kerosene in the back of the shed. After tugging on jeans and a flannel shirt. After lacing up her boots. After dragging the chair out the back door and over to the garden near the brush pile.

To her it was all one fluid motion, one clear thought: burn the chair.

Her elderly neighbor Chuck ambled over. He had picked some late raspberries and offered up a bright handful. Mellow and sweet. "They taste like a first kiss," Jackie said, and then she blushed a little. Chuck examined the site. The chair, the kerosene, the matches Jackie held firmly in her hand.

"Had enough of that chair, I see," Chuck said. He took a few steps back, looking unsure of Jackie's aim with the kerosene. She struck a match, set it to the letter, and then the chair's arm. She marveled at how quickly the entire thing was aflame, alive, almost, in its burning.

"Never settle on a chair," Jackie said. "Wait for just the right one, even if it costs you twice as much." She folded her arms across her chest. "Nobody approved of that chair."

"I've had a few of those over the years," Chuck said. "It's worth the effort of getting rid of them."

Jackie nodded. Together, they watched the flames lap up near the apple tree's branches.

"So, he's not coming home anytime soon?" Chuck said. "Owen, I mean."

An ex-marine, Chuck had taken it upon himself to check in on Jackie at least three times a week. Soon they were exchanging recipes and gardening magazines. Friends in that unlikely way a neighbor can become a lottery win.

"Owen. Owen who?" Jackie asked, staring at the flames.

Chuck creaked away after a time. He held out his hand for the matches before he left. "I could use a few of those at home," he said.

Jackie laid the pack in his smooth palm. The chair's peak had passed, its flames withering to a smoulder. Black char. Innards. Springs. Flecks of the letter rose up as if called to heaven.

Jackie watched Chuck maneuver his back porch steps. She could see his glance through the kitchen window and his dim kitchen light. Fall was here. Jackie could feel it eating at her bones. The apples would soon be ready—little, plump Cortlands, only good for a few short weeks before they turned to mush.

Looking for a Sign

Maria's heart aches as she sips her morning coffee—the mug a burden. The tidy houseplants on the windowsill stare her down just like the old ladies on the bus. She drums her fingers, kicks a slippered foot forward, forward, forward. Her world had been full of friends and love. Now she's landed here where only sunlight trickles through her doorway.

At night she settles onto her back—sheets snug to her chin—and watches the cars' headlights travel, twist, and turn on her ceiling, escape out the window, return. And then a moment of divine, dreamless sleep before morning.

Maria traces the curve of her hips, the angle of the throw pillows in the living room, the edge of a houseplant's leaf.

Caravan, Suburbia

There goes the rickety caravan—rambling through the front yard. It knocks over the potted mum and rocks on the dented lawn as it passes the flagpole. The front wheels creak. I spot some cleavage, the thinning, ratty wool pants. My automatic porch light clicks on then off as it passes.

My cat jumps off my lap, runs to the front door and sits, looking intent and in love with what she knows is just beyond. I fold up the recliner, look through the picture window. There's just some distant laughter I'm probably imagining, a moon, and the solitary birdbath with its calm waters, smooth sides.

As I open the door and the cat bolts free, I gather in the smell of wood smoke, raw upturned earth, the quick scent of passion, and one low, unsung note abandoned in the stray leaves.

Singing Cowboy, Dayton, Ohio

Kenny pulled an old Holiday Inn towel from his camera bag to wipe the sweat from the pony. He quickly rubbed her face and sides. Puff stomped her hooves and made a strange, yet personal, whinnying noise.

Kenny adjusted his cowboy hat and made sure the knot in his bandanna rested on his left shoulder. He flicked a bug from his neatly pressed white T-shirt, tugged at the knees of his stiff Wranglers, and walked himself and Puff the pony up Mr. H. John Smith's sidewalk, past his well-manicured lawn and peonies.

Kenny whispered to himself, "You are a photographer. You are a salesman. You are a cowboy," then he rang Mr. H. John Smith's bell. It chimed with orchestral harmony. H.J. himself opened the door.

Kenny inhaled. The pony snorted.

Kenny said, "Howdy there, Mr. H. John Smith. I'm a cowboy

photographer, taking rough and rowdy shots of children or grand-children on the back of trusty Silver here, my cowboy steed."

H.J. smiled a serene, senile smile—a smile that suggested he had all the time in the world. He quietly said, "Hello. My name is John Smith. What's your name?"

Kenny did not have all the time in the world. He worked on commission. He removed a tiny ball of lint from his jeaned knee. He wiped at the spot once, twice.

"Well, I'm Bob Buckaroo. And I'm wondering if you have any little pardners you'd like to put on my trusty horse here? A grandson, or a pet?"

Recently, Kenny had photographed a dachshund and a cockatoo perched atop Puff.

H.J.'s blue eyes remained steady. "Won't you please come in and sit down while I get my checkbook?"

Kenny stood in the doorway, awkwardly holding Puff's reins. The checkbook didn't come into play until a few weeks after the shoot when he brought the prints around.

H.J. said, "By all means, bring Silver in too. Sure, pull her right in. That's it. Shut that screen door behind you, there. Make yourself at home. Now what did you say your full name was?"

Kenny said, "Bob. Bob Buckaroo."

The first PowerPoint screen in the Pony Express Photography two-week training session warned future cowboy photographers in all caps to never tell the client your real name.

In his opening remarks, Jim B. Manscot, owner and found-er of the Pony Express Photography Corporation, said, "You are a cowboy. A cowboy photographer." He said it over and over again. He also made it clear cowboy photographers did not drink on the job and that they cleaned their own horses and their fingernails—in that order.

Kenny sat at the kitchen table. He tried to cross his ankles but his spurs tangled. Instead he spread his legs wide apart, put his hat on one knee, his camera bag on the other. He dabbed his forehead with a neatly folded handkerchief from his back pocket.

Puff stood contentedly in the large foyer. Kenny had grown to love his assigned pony. He had heard horror stories about some of the other animals—wandering out into traffic, biting children, eating cats. But not Puffy. Puffy loved Kenny, and Kenny loved Puffy.

H.J. returned from the refrigerator with lemonade and a check made out to Bob Buckaroo for twenty-five dollars.

"Now when does my subscription begin?"

Kenny looked at Puff, then at H.J. He cleared his throat. "I'm not selling magazines there, Bronc," he said. "I'm taking authentic, unique, one-of-a-kind western photos."

H.J. stood up straight, stared off beyond the wall clock for a second. Then he said, "Oh. I forgot the apple for Silver." He cleared his throat. "How thoughtless of me." He petted Puff on the nose.

Kenny sighed and looked at his watch. It had stirrups hanging down either side of his wrist. He had received it at the Pony Express awards banquet for the biggest single sale in one month.

He remembered Steve and Steve well. A handsome couple, they just couldn't stop posing, telling Kenny he was the cutest cowboy they'd ever seen. They sent him a bottle of champagne after they got their prints.

H.J. rustled in the refrigerator again and came back with an apple. He looked Puff in the eye and said, "Hi-Ho." Puff daintily plucked the Granny Smith from his hand and chewed thoughtfully at Kenny.

H.J. leaned against the wall and folded his arms across his chest. He said, "I used to be a cowboy myself. In Wyoming. There weren't any cowboys in Ohio when I moved here, you know. Especially not in Dayton."

Kenny nodded. He stood up, settling his jeans back over his boots by tugging at each knee. "Yesirree. It's amazing how times have changed. Now cowboys pop up everywhere. Why, just turn the corner these days and, blam, there's another cowboy for ya."

H.J. nodded, thinking this over.

Kenny said, "So, Mr. Smith, do you have any little critters here at your house?" He tried to peek into the next room, hoping there might be a more receptive, better grounded, Mrs. H.J. Smith.

"I was a cowboy in Wyoming, rounded up dogies and whistled carefree. What a life, I'll tell you. What a goddamn life."

Kenny cleared his throat. "You have a dog then?" He knocked his hat off the table as he asked the question. As he picked it up, he scanned its neatly brushed surface for stray pet hairs.

H.J. looked at Kenny and his hat for a long time. He said, "Dogies are stray calves, Bob. Surely you know that. Has cowboying changed that much?"

H.J. shook his head and looked out the kitchen window at the brightly flickering leaves on the trees in his yard. He said, "Things just can't have changed that much."

Kenny said, "Oh. Sorry there." He wiped his forehead again. A big ball of concern swelled in his stomach, it expanded the slower H.J. talked.

H.J. said, "In Wyoming," he looked Kenny in the eye, "in Wyoming, the sky is so big you find out what it means to be a real man, Buck."

Kenny nodded, "Yes sir." He made a mental note to remember to pick up the dry cleaning on the way home. Patty had asked him to do that for the past three days running.

"Ever been to Wyoming, Bob Buckaroo?"

"Well. No sir."

"Then you don't know what it means to be a real man, do you, Bob?" H.J. smiled a sad, watery smile. He unfolded his arms and turned to look at Puff, one hand leaning on his door, his back to Kenny.

Kenny said, "Well, I guess not."

"The stars are everywhere there, Buck. I swear you could pick up a rock and there'd be a star just as quiet as could be lying under it. It's different in Ohio. Stars aren't everywhere here. They're right there in the sky. Easy. In Wyoming, it's a whole different story. Being lonely means something in a state like Wyoming."

H.J. reached to stroke Puff softly down her neck.

Kenny finished his lemonade, gulping it quickly hoping to flush away the lump sitting now like soggy cardboard in his middle. He set the empty glass on the table. "Yes. So H.J., how about an authentic cowboy picture then? You on Silver there? For old roping and riding's sake?"

H.J. looked at Kenny, then he looked out the window again. "Would you and Silver excuse me a minute?" H.J. took Kenny's glass to the sink, rinsed it, then walked slowly up his carpeted stairs.

Kenny knew he wasted valuable time on calls like this. He guessed it went without saying that under no circumstances should a cowboy photographer bring his pony into a client's home. He could see lawsuits popping up like spring flowers. Kenny jingle-jangled past Puff into H.J.'s den saying, "Stupid, stupid, stupid," under his breath. Down the street probably lived a doctor with ten well-be-haved kids dying to be photographed five times each.

He calculated the commission, then stopped and hit himself in the head muttering, "Calm. Calm. Calm."

Colonial furniture and hardwood floors decorated H.J.'s rustic den. A mounted deer head stared at Kenny, each of its feet turned neatly upward into hat racks. A beveled glass mirror centered under the doe's head. Kenny checked his hair. He tried without much success to fluff the hat head out. Kenny thought about how much Steve and Steve would have paid for that deer-head and hat-rack combo. He reached up to pet the deer's nose.

Kenny heard spurs coming down the stairs. He turned and there stood H.J.: chaps, leather, fringe, flannel, hat, spurs, and boots.

H.J. said softly, "Let's go get 'em, Buck."

Dollar signs lit up in front of Kenny like neon at dusk. He yelled, "Yee-haw!"

His luck was turning like a chicken on a spit. He hadn't made a sale all day. He heard they gave an authentic replica Pony Express blanket if you got the sales award two years in a row. He hoped he had enough film.

Kenny led Puff outside and stood her near the fence in H.J.'s yard. H.J. sauntered over, impressive. He had a remarkable physique for an old, senile guy.

"Ya-hoo!" Kenny yelled. His camera shutter flew. H.J. on the pony, beside the pony, with hat on, hat off.

Kenny said, "H.J. You've made this cowboy's day."

"Ride the range, Buck," H.J. said. "Ride it true."

As Kenny shot the last pictures of his last roll of film, he noticed the sun slanting deep yellow across the lawn. Nearly four-thirty, he'd have to hurry to meet the trailer that took him and Puff and all the other cowboy photographers roaming the neighborhood home.

Kenny wanted one more shot featuring the holster H.J. had buckled low on his hips.

Kenny said, "H.J. Get those guns out for this last one. That's it." He kneeled to get rays of sun shooting like a wagon wheel around H.J.'s head. He said, "Shoot 'em straight up. Yeah like that."

H.J. hesitated but pointed the guns up—one slightly higher than the other. He smiled.

Kenny took the shot. "Great," he said. "Really great. Yes." He had a good feeling that one would make the cover of the newsletter.

Kenny shoved his camera into his bag. He knew those years in high school photography club would pay off. "That was really amazing. Thanks. Thanks a lot, H.J. Well, adios. Silver and I have to hightail it out of here. I'll bring these over in a few weeks for you to review." Kenny leaned over to shake H.J.'s hand.

The look of confusion returned to H.J.'s face. His puzzlement seemed to clear, then he pointed the gun in his right hand at Kenny.

Kenny backed up with his extended hand up in the air. He said, "Whoa there, pardner." Kenny laughed softly. Then he remembered the dead deer in the den. He picked up his camera bag—tried to make eye contact with Puff.

H.J. held the gun back down at his side. He said, "You're not a cowboy, Buck."

Kenny said, "Oh yes I am, H.J. I'm a red-blooded American cowboy." He didn't want to sound indignant, but he could hear the same tone that always got him in trouble with his mother-in-law at family dinners.

H.J. moved toward Kenny, "Why not admit it, Bob. Say, 'I'm not a cowboy.' Sometimes it's important to face up to the truth of things."

Kenny walked backward, got tripped up in his spurs, and fell onto his back with a soft thump.

H.J. stood over Kenny, his shadow hovering over him. He looked majestic in the late afternoon light. "Buck, cowboys don't roam the suburbs of Dayton. They round animals up, Buck, in the country. Every goddamn cowboy in his right mind knows that."

"Well, clearly not every cowboy, H.J.," Kenny said. "Not every single one."

H.J. seemed to stand taller, unflinching. He pointed the gun in his right hand at Kenny again.

Kenny couldn't quite figure how he'd gotten himself into this situation. He remembered eating Grape-Nuts in the morning. He'd had a grilled cheese and side salad for lunch. He'd led a good life. He'd forgotten the dry cleaning, but he was going to get that tonight on his way home.

H.J. calmly moved his legs into a wider and more becoming stance.

Kenny could feel moisture seeping into his T-shirt. He would miss loading Puffy into the trailer. He would die in suburbia dressed as a cowboy with his spurs embedded in the lawn of a senile bronco buster. He knew his mother would never forgive him—that Patty would remarry and start taking Pilates classes on a regular basis. Kenny wiggled first one spur free, then another.

H.J. sighed, looked down the empty block one way, then the other. He focused on a point far off on the horizon.

Kenny wondered about H.J.'s neighbors. From the looks of

it they'd have nice office jobs and Cadillacs.

H.J. moved his finger from the trigger he'd been massaging. He took a deep breath, then another, and let out the most impressive, and only, yodel Kenny had ever heard in person in his life. It traveled down the flat street, bounced off two-car garages and maple trees. Kenny figured H.J.'s friends in Wyoming probably heard it too.

Black-and-white images of cows and campfires blurred in Kenny's head. Old Western movies from the Sunday afternoons of his youth came rushing in. They got mixed with Frankie and Annette on the beach and Gene Autry singing on a horse, riding into the sunset.

H.J. gathered himself together, cocked the pistol, and aimed again.

Kenny sat up, his arms slouched between his outspread legs. H.J. held that shiny, silver gun with the steadiest hand Kenny had ever seen on an old man. Just as Kenny thought to himself that H.J. looked too confident, he pulled the trigger. Kenny let out a high, girlish shriek.

There was a quick bang, then silence. Puff whinnied. A breeze swung through the trees, rippling the water in the birdbath as a few cardinals took flight.

Kenny wasn't hurt, wounded, or in pain. Some thoughtful grandson or daughter had put caps or blanks or something—but not bullets—in crazy H.J.'s guns.

H.J. took a deep breath. He helped Kenny up. He said, "Just say it, Buck."

Kenny said, "What?" He put his hands on his hips in disgust. "Say what?" He picked grass clumps from his spurs, shooed a fly from his face. He pulled on his T-shirt to look at the grass stain.

H.J. said, "Say 'I'm not a cowboy.'"

With a snotty contempt he could no longer try to disguise, Kenny said, "I'm not a cowboy. There. Happy?"

H.J. said, his eyes half-shut, "Say it louder."

A few cars turned down H.J.'s road. Finally, the neighbors returned from their normal, hectic days behind desks with copy machines and computer screens, easing their sedans into their driveways with confidence.

H.J. said, "Say 'I'm a low-life salesman.'"

Kenny looked at H.J. Without hesitation, he said, "I'm a low-life salesman."

H.J. said, "Once more."

Kenny gritted his teeth. "My name is Kenny," he said. "That's Puff. She's not a horse. She's a pony. I'm a low-life salesman dressed like a stupid cowboy. And I regret it. I regret it all."

"Thank you, pardner," H.J. said. "You've made me feel much better. Now get off my property before I count to ten."

From then on everything happened in slow motion. H.J. chanted, "Three . . . Four . . . Five . . ." Puff nodded her head up and down, up and down. Kenny tugged her out of H.J.'s peonies, pulled her onto the road.

After fitting one pistol snugly into his holster, H.J. drew the other from his left hip. He aimed at the ceramic caterpillar in his flower garden and blew it to bits.

H.J. blew on the gun and pushed back his hat. With narrow hips, he sauntered up to his screen door, singing softly, *I'm a Pistol Packin' Papa. I roam from town to town* . . . He turned at the door. "If you kept your nose clean there Kenny, you wouldn't get yourself into these situations." The door tapped shut behind him.

Suddenly, it was like H.J. never existed. Birds chirped. A squirrel scampered up a drainpipe. Kenny fought the urge to faint. Instead he walked. His legs shook and his spurs were bent. The sun set off in the distance in bright oranges and purples.

He considered how he would explain the suspicious grass stains on his back to Patty as Puff trotted slowly, trustfully, beside him. Kenny stopped and hugged her. She nuzzled his chin. He twisted himself up into her saddle unsure of what came next. Puff moved forward in a straight, steady line continuing on Oakville Road past Third and Fourth until she came to Fifth where she made a left. Kenny didn't even hold the reins.

A Crowd

1. JOSHUA IN TOWN

Joshua Stevenson harbored secrets—dark corners angled in his memories like rusty levers. Some days he knew this, but other days he lived his life as if nothing had ever happened to him. His tide of believing pulled and pushed. He kept his dark world organized. But still, images developed like a musty photo. They played like a crackly movie reel he couldn't get to focus.

Joshua knew Susan only by sight. She claimed the corner table at the café every Wednesday morning. Joshua poured coffee, cut slices of tart for customers. He watched Susan as she organized her manila folders, chewed the end of her pen, ate a wheat roll without butter, her dainty pinkie finger pointing upward with each bite.

One day, during a lull, Susan stopped her fidgeting with this and that piece of paper and looked straight at him. Joshua's insides lit up. He smiled, and Susan walked to the case, leaned in toward his flip of curly hair, and said, "Stop it, Mr. Counterperson." She tapped the glass twice, returned to her cluttered life, not looking up again.

"Do you think she meant the staring?" Joshua later asked Frankie, his coworker.

Frankie laughed. "I don't think she was talking about you cleaning the coffee maker, man." Frankie nudged his thick black glasses up his nose, adjusted the zipper on his hoodie to mid-chest. "You're kind of freaky with your eavesdropping. Just don't look at people so much. I mean, either that or ask her out."

Joshua folded cake boxes, one after another, as he considered his possibilities.

Days passed. He didn't see Susan on Wednesdays anymore. He suspected she found a new café or moved to a new regular day outside of his schedule. He occupied himself with other people, thought about other stuff, like his inability to ask out girls like Susan. Like his habit of making friends with hipsters who annoyed him.

Frankie kneeled down to tie his sneakers and rubbed his eyes, the dark circles distinct and tender underneath. "Man, you just have stuff wrong," he said. "There are all these wonderful people in the world, and you just go right for the ones that fuck you up. I mean, what's wrong with you?"

Joshua knew what was wrong with him. The sum of his past made him move in the wrong emotional direction over and over again. Every so often he'd see a hand fly up in his hazy memory. A door slam. He'd smell bacon frying and hear a childhood whimper. Everything would fade to black, and then he'd take his fifteen-minute break. Outside, he'd smoke a cigarette. The opening of the pack, the pounding of the pack against his left palm, the drawing out of a slender stick—it helped him focus on the simple world around him. He'd tuck the other problems back into their hiding places. Smoke. Push through the café's door, tie on his apron.

One day he saw Susan walking out of the grocery store on Third Street, two paper sacks crunched in her arms. Then she was in line ahead of him at a double feature. Always alone, this Susan. Head down, thoughtful, never rushing as she walked the river trail. Her life continued without him. Not that Joshua had been in her life—but still. There was Susan walking in the park, hands in the pockets of a red trench coat.

Joshua said hello one day, waved, tried to get her attention. Susan turned to him after she'd placed her order at the corner deli, and he told her he'd stopped what he was doing in his head. He said he'd taken her advice.

Susan looked thoughtful for a second and then said, "Important step." She fiddled with her hair, smiled, grabbed her sandwich, wrapped up neatly in white paper and fastened with a piece of masking tape, and walked away.

Eventually, Joshua quit the café, as hard as it was to leave the easy routine of opening the shop, pouring coffee, ringing up sales, and flipping chairs onto tables at closing time. He needed to move on before he made a mistake.

For a while, he lived off savings. Just took a few weeks to think about something other than Susan's brown hair, her slender fingers scribbling notes. He walked the streets, nodding to old customers, sometimes stopping in the café to say hi to everyone.

His head cleared in those in-between days. He had a kind of confidence he'd lose altogether in the future, but for now he could see firmly what his life was and was not. And then, one day, far off in the distance down an alleyway, Susan in her red coat. She crooked one tiny finger to pull him in.

2. FRANKIE

Not particularly smart or substantially good looking, Frankie kept to the corners. He browsed the produce at the local grocer, was disappointed with the pears and then the peaches.

He never saw it coming—it being happiness, it being disappointment. It being Hallie with her rose-scented hair and Dansko clogs.

But then, it was too late. Frankie was a check-out girl's memory, an old man with a cane.

3. SUSAN

This is my backyard before all the fruit trees went crooked. Back before the three cement deer and the overgrown vegetable garden. It's windy. I'm wearing the plaid cape my cousin Kimmy handed down. The cape is red. The clouds are low. I have a small paper kite in my hand. Blue, orange, and yellow construction paper glued to yarn. The fringe on the cape rises and settles with the chilly gusts. The ground is cold and difficult under my feet.

I imagine that speck in the window is my mother watching me.

My kite droops and hangs in the wind. I actually think it will fly. I spin around and around like a wooden top. I wait to totter to the ground. I wait.

The clouds are low.

4. BABY

The smell of coffee creeped through the campground. Next, the pine and moist dirt. Susan opened her eyes to see the dome of their tent stretched taut against the poles. Camping, she thought. State Parks, she thought. Sex in the woods, she thought. She waited for her husband to crawl awkwardly through, smiling. Zippers buzzing good morning. Two blue enameled tin cups in his hands.

IV

Silence, Pushing

E lizabeth wanted a dog. Now that she hid away in her room most days, it seemed like the right thing to do. They'd get her a puppy, and she would engage with them again. These days, Charley and Jane used words like "engage" in their daily conversations where they used to say things like "talk."

But they weren't thinking "engage" as they buckled themselves into the car on a sunny October day, sneaking glimpses of Elizabeth's profile as she leaned against the backseat door, tipped her head against the window as if she wished to push herself out. She watched the scenery rush past her with the emptiest deep blue eyes.

Since late August Jane and Charley had begun whispering quietly in their bedroom late at night, sure that Elizabeth might hear them. She seemed to sniff out their every intention. "It's like she's psychic," Jane said, and then felt a kind of shame shiver down her spine. She didn't like her daughter much these days, and she couldn't admit that to anyone. Not to Charley, not to the women on her tennis team, or the ladies at the coffee shop who all seemed to adore their children—seemed to find their impossible adolescent behavior amusing.

It did seem though that Jane's friends knew things about Elizabeth they weren't telling her. The women talked cautiously over practice volleys or steaming lattes. "How is Elizabeth doing now?" Suzy asked. "A free spirit can be tough," said Tania.

What Elizabeth did these days when she wasn't home was a mystery to Jane. No more dance lessons. No more track team. Graffiti, most likely, since Elizabeth had covered her bedroom walls with letters and symbols. And drugs, maybe, too. Elizabeth had blossomed and then took a strange and sudden detour. Now she fumed and hated. Everything. Absolutely everything. Charley's eyes teared up when he looked through the old photo albums. "Where did we go wrong?" he asked one night when he knew Jane pretended to sleep. "Where did my little girl go?" he whispered.

"Charley, we have become the Afterschool Specials we watched as kids," Jane said back from her pillow. "We're the dumb, clueless parents. Presto." She pretend-snapped her fingers and immediately regretted her tone, the acid flush all her words had these days. Jane lay awake the rest of the night listening to the house settle around her, wondering if it really was the house settling around her, if she should check Elizabeth's room. Feeling old and regretful. Morning soon spit birdsong at her.

When the day arrived for traveling the sunny winding hills of West Virginia to pick up the puppy, Charley announced to Elizabeth, "It'll be an adventure!" Their daughter brooded over the toaster. To punctuate the silence that followed, Elizabeth's waffles popped up like a jack-in-the-box. She crammed one into her mouth like a prisoner. "What?" she asked. "Are you guys going out of town?"

They told her about the idea. The puppy. And it's true her eyes transformed nearly to the child they'd known. Elizabeth smiled and squealed and almost hugged Charley but stopped herself. "You aren't kidding, right?" she said.

"No, no," he said. "A dog, a puppy. We think you're ready."

They all piled into the car. Silence pushed them forward after they wouldn't let Elizabeth play her rap station. Later there wasn't any radio reception anyway.

The puppies in the small plastic swimming pool set up in Mrs. Francine Edwards' living room wrestled and squirmed. Mrs. Edwards loved dogs, that was clear from her knickknacks and her sweatshirt and the framed cross-stitches lining the walls. "God bless our Hounds," one read in green and blue. "(Wo)man's best friend," proclaimed another. "I love dogs," she said.

"I can see that," Charley said. Elizabeth giggled, actually giggled. Then she quickly picked an all-black puppy without too much consideration, Jane thought. Jane did think the puppy seemed wise, and yes, she too secretly loved the little guy's bright red tongue with one little black spot in the middle. Elizabeth said the dog was cool. She cradled it under her arm. She named the dog Tip.

Elizabeth wouldn't let Tip out of her sight those first weeks. She doted on him, trained him. She took him for long walks.

The parents thought they had finally done something right. Jane even ventured to mention the dog to her friends, and the women all agreed that sometimes children just needed a pal. That maybe the dog would turn Elizabeth around. And Jane wondered—around from what?

Elizabeth had been sneaking out at night for months. She had been skipping school and was now failing every subject. There were the cigarettes they found, and then the joint in the back pocket of her jeans, then the pills in her knapsack, the smeared spray paint on a blue bandana. But still, this just seemed like normal teenaged rebellion. They would confront her and reconcile.

Jane and Charley entered her room together, bound in love, still. Kind people, really. A bit naive, they realized. None of the parenting books had prepared them for anything.

They entered Elizabeth's once-pink room, now splashed with a language they couldn't read. Elizabeth was wound into her beanbag chair, staring blankly at the puppy as it nipped at a toy shaped like a squirrel, growling at it and then pouncing and skittering away.

Jane didn't know why a wave of terror shot up her spine. Later she would remember this moment as the point from which they could not turn back. "Elizabeth," she said. "You're grounded. We're taking your house keys. We're locking your door from the outside every night."

Elizabeth looked up at them, past them, her eyes focusing on a time and place far beyond this one. "I'll just crawl out the window," she sighed.

The puppy pounced its way toward Charley, absently tugged on the toy. The dog whined, then gave a small bark. Elizabeth's eyes unfolded from the deep dark nothing.

"Shut up," she said to the dog, looking at her parents. "God. Why is everyone so stupid?"

"Now Elizabeth. Be nice," Charley said as if he was talking to a much younger Elizabeth. He scooted the puppy toward her, nudging its little black bottom with his big hand. The puppy's over-sized paws galumphed it forward, his head tipped toward Elizabeth, its sleek black fur so soft—Jane knew this—just between the ears.

Then Elizabeth picked up her puppy and threw it hard across the room.

The future came at Jane like a dust storm. She had to squint to see through. The arrest, the detention center, the detox, the therapists, the boarding school, the regrets, the apologies, the relapse.

Later, much later, when that time had reduced down to simmering white noise, Jane knew the sound the puppy made against the wall should have been much louder.

Secrets

I t might have happened this way: Robbie jumped out of the hayloft and hit his head. Or, he was pushed out of the hayloft and hit his head. Or, he was goaded out. The fact is: he fell out and hit his head, and they all agreed it wise not to tell their mother.

High up in the hayloft, Robbie had looked down on the pile of fresh hay. The sweet smells; stark blue skies creating infinity outside the barn door. The air sparkled with dust lit by scattered sun rays through the barn's sagging walls, and his brothers romped all around. Hand-me-downs, crew cuts, hard-soled shoes.

Robbie wondered at the pile of hay, and then everyone looked over the edge—like looking into the future. Endless and fun.

So they jumped. Robbie wasn't the first, but perhaps the biggest. And somehow—whether he decided or was decided upon—he found himself floating up above the mound, suspended for an instant, legs cartwheeling, his mind blank and full of stars.

Then he plunged down through the scratchy mess, and the floor rose up to meet him like a promise. He hit the floor and his head, his spine clinking. Inventing problems for the not now.

But for now Robbie lay stretched out—spread-eagle—trying to make himself into an ocean. His younger brother falling, like an angel, from the sky.

Oklahoma Men

In Oklahoma, men drink their coffee black. It costs fifteen cents and comes in small Styrofoam cups the color of Elmer's Glue, the color of new light bulbs.

They don't slurp or blow. The coffee remains as placid as a lake.

Tea is not served.

Younger men add sugar. They do this by opening two stiff packets at once. The grains pour slowly into the dark liquid, settling like trusting pioneers in the bottom of their cups. In this way, they know something dark and sweet is always waiting.

The men sit around square tables in the early, early morning, in corner cafés called Karen's or Jake's or The Bluebird. Fluorescent lights hum, while baseball hats with feed company logos reach from one pink temple to the next. Out back, big green pickup trucks tick and settle.

When the men speak, it's in four-part harmony. They wear leather boots that creak. They eat donuts and never turn quickly on one another or brush crumbs onto the floor.

As the sun trips across the checked linoleum they talk about how things were—how much harder everyone worked—how much harder they must work now. The men look at the front of their hands, then they look at the back. They settle in their seats like hard rubber. They push their hats back on their heads to see clearly across their days, across hills and miles, across all the fences they've strung together to know where they've been, to know how to get back to what it was they started.

Locusts

I want him to go away, leave like the locusts did after they heaved their ugly bodies down and destroyed everything. After the locusts left, there was silence and peace. You could hear things you couldn't before—the smallest sounds seemed beautiful and sweet. Water trickling echoed for hours. Doing nothing, just not struggling, was the nicest thing.

I wanted the locusts to leave—to rise and descend no more. I wanted them to rise up in a buzzing clatter and leave the fields of my life. I want him to quietly take his stuff from my apartment. To walk up my stairs then back down. Or if not, I want the locusts to return to take it all, to rise up with everything bundled tight to their stuffed bodies. I want them to ascend in search of all they have yet to find.

Then when he asks where everything is, I'll say I'm not sure, probably somewhere over Kansas by now.

What If the Locusts Returned?

O f course this has nothing to do with locusts. It really has nothing to do with me. It's you.

You come and sit—peeling the soggy label off your beer. There's mud on your boots. You sit at my kitchen table until I can't hear my own heart beating, until I can't hear the spoon I've been tapping against my dinner plate. Until I throw the spoon neatly into the sink. The clatter it makes is the bell that rings at the carnival when the hammer is raised and lowered just right. There's a pause. Expectation. And the bell rings. The spoon clatters.

I say, "What the hell?" or "Why in the hell?"

The word "hell" is definitely in there one way or another.

And you. You look up with your bug eyes surprised and moist. You rub your hands together, and I know you'll either grab your coat and go or you'll sit there and say something that sounds important.

And now I'm supposed to know what it is you say. But already it's getting dark in my kitchen, in my living room, and my bedroom. The ice is melting in my tall tumbler. And it's so damn silent.

Full Moon

Two babies, twins. One cup of coffee. Everything here is mine: sink, dishes, stove, babies, mug. It's all steaming and fresh. I'm not supposed to drink coffee—not now while I'm locked in the moist life of nursing. But I deserve it. And the twins deserve their sleep. We're all indulging ourselves after what we've been through.

They have each other, and I have this coffee. Already, I'm on the outside of their lives looking in, trying to see how it will crescendo: the apartment expanding, the stove's four burners all going at once, the sun rising, another full moon, the mug chipping, the coffee growing cold.

I sneeze. The twins settle like a pile of twigs.

Home

The quiet house and abandoned tangerine peels. The hi-fi equipment, dusty. The runner along the stairs. Matching doilies on the arms of the rocking chair and where my head rests. Books—hard leather spines cracking in the bookcases with glass doors. A pantry. Jars of jams. Beets and tomatoes pulsing. An empty clothesline in the backyard. A garden with more vegetables than I'll ever eat. A doghouse I don't go near because of the hornet's nest.

Trees

The trees are a stark horizon. They are skinny men in ill-fitting suits selling bibles, impossible brooms stood on end so the cats won't eat the thistles.

They're deep sea creatures, scraggily haired women who've had one too many perms. They are the anorexic cheerleaders, waving their ghost arms chanting: Go! Go!

Still Life

Harry Kane matched up the seams of his cuffed trousers and lay them across the back of a chair. He had worn them to his internship that morning, and then to the desultory going away party for Katy, and on to the hardware store on Main Street for a new blind for the back window. He'd chosen a tan, airy thing woven out of fragile sticks with a cloth string to pull it up and down. He installed the blind with the two hooks included in the package and stepped back to admire his handiwork. It looked good. Like Hawaii even though he'd never been there. The Tropics. Right there in his home. He imagined it swaying with the breeze next spring when the windows were open. It would permit a soft filtered light into the tiny back sunroom.

Later, as dusk turned to night and the street sounds muffled and ceased, Harry opened the bottle of whiskey he'd stopped to buy after the blind.

He set his drink down on a coaster that said LEE'S HARD-WARE STORE and he picked up his pants again from the back of the chair. He matched up the seams of his trousers again and carefully folded them—waist to cuffs, knees to waist. He placed the pants on the corner of his desk in the front room of his tiny cottage. The new blind hung limp and dark down the hallway.

Harry's blue dress shirt hung loose to the middle of his boxers. He'd ironed it that morning with the sturdy board that was fitted into his kitchen wall. Now the shirt showed the day's wear. It was a fine shirt—good quality with a tiny X-pattern replicated in the cotton weave. He often received compliments when he wore it to work at the firm. He couldn't remember if anyone had said anything today.

Catching himself in the mirror, Harry studied his scrawny chicken legs and bony knees. He rarely wore shorts—even in the dead of summer. He unbuttoned his shirt and slid out of it, folded it like his mother had taught him, turning back its arms, angling the bottom into itself, and then again, smoothing it flat with his thin fingers.

The bottle of whiskey sat half-empty now on the other end of the desk, but he didn't feel a thing different. Harry liked its caramel glow, lit by his desk lamp beside the pile of neatly folded clothes. The blue shirt looked good, he thought, on top of the tan pants like that. He adjusted the tip of the collar, smoothed the soft cotton again.

He finished off the whiskey in his tumbler, set his thick glass next to the bottle. It was a nice little still life he had going. He glanced at the blind at the end of the hallway. He couldn't help imagining the world outside through the blackness that had descended on his town. The shops had closed hours earlier, locked up their front doors with swift clicks and tugs. He imagined a few lost-pet flyers loosened from telephone poles and cartwheeling down the sidewalk. Hazy yellow streetlights blinked on here and there. Porchlights had long ago clicked off as each occupant found home base, turned on the TV, reheated leftovers on rotating plates in microwaves. He imagined leaves rustling, branches shaking themselves along the roads. He poured more whiskey, took a sip, the heat of it sliding down his throat.

He was in The Now. He knew that—recognized it from the other times. He pulled off his boxers, folded them in half and then in half again, followed by his white T-shirt and black socks. He balled the socks and placed them like a tiny torpedo on top of the pile.

Harry now stood naked in the middle of his small, immaculate living space.

The clock read 3:00 a.m.

He checked to make sure the burners on the stove were off.

Harry pushed open the front door and then stood there with his arms at his sides: 3:05.

Take the first step, he thought. And so he did. The keys to his front door in his left hand. His right hand still clutched the doorknob. He dropped the keys beside that morning's newspaper. The streetlight shone on the keys, and Harry admired the glint before stepping off his frayed welcome mat and onto the cool cement that felt like sandpaper scratching under the balls and heels of his feet. Leaves raged from the branches as far as he could see down the road, both directions—red, gold, a luscious cocoa brown—countless more of them on the ground. Color smothering everything even in the dark.

The trees' silhouetted arms sang hallelujah. The leaves clapped. Harry walked down Maple Street. Dark houses, the faint muffled dog bark, a settling *tick tick* of a foundation. An electronic hum ebbed under everything, coursed through him. The town shut down for the night, but tilted toward morning.

Harry followed along Maple to where it intersected Grove at the old schoolyard. Empty and hollow. The ball field pulsed like a lush, green symbol of something Harry couldn't name. He continued on through the neighborhood, damp leaves sticking to the bottoms of his feet, his goose-pimpled skin alive, separate from him—alert. His testicles and penis swaying between his legs as he walked.

His brain followed his progress from above somehow, tracking him like a satellite.

The railyard. Six or seven blocks. Harry climbed a scrubby embankment, picking over the ragged gravel that would've hurt his feet any other day. Air swelled around him. Harry's nipples rose taut and firm, tiny rosebuds on his chest. The moon hid behind clouds. A streetlight spotlit the heaps of used railroad ties, scattered like giant matchsticks. Harry walked into the half-shadow, sat down in between the two sets of thick, glossy railroad tracks.

From above he could see himself, a small naked man, his shoulders curved, knees bent, sitting between the rails that stretched from here to everywhere. Beautiful, Harry thought.

So full, his past. It raised a static in his head that buzzed like flies, subsided, and started up again.

That his clothes were neatly piled back home comforted Harry. He thought about his mother, widowed, soon to outlive her only son. This fact flashed through Harry's brain without any conviction. He remembered his mother from a time long ago, before all these complications. Her smile then, her creamy skin, her slender finger rubbing his cheek. He remembered his boyhood dog Ralphy scampering in circles every time Harry returned home. He remembered the apple tree across the street from his childhood home. The little dried-up fruit it plopped onto the lawn each summer. *Thump, thump* onto the ground. He thought about the phone ringing, and his father dying and then dead in his mother's arms.

And then his thoughts tumbled again, a rumbling mess of sense and nonsense recalibrating itself. He sat curled in between the two rails like a blown leaf, his arms around his knees, his forehead resting there—face tucked down.

He felt the train before he could hear it. The vibration like an earthquake under his feet, up his backside, knocking at his vertebrae. The sound shook him like a monster that knew Harry waited there for him. The monster raced to meet Harry, it filled his eardrums. The sky rattled, the Earth itself shook. *Forgiveness* was a word that came to him. It flashed across his brain italicized. He realized he didn't understand the word. Suddenly it was a foreign concept. It flew by in his thoughts again like one of those advertisements pulled behind an airplane above the baseball stadium, and then erased by the roar of the monster. It rolled within his boiling thoughts.

The monster's powerful engine turned the train wheels and the wheels ground along the rails. The whistle blew once, twice, then two more times in quick succession.

The wind rose, a rushing trauma shoving up behind him, sharp and cold. Pebbles, soot, and dirt, little flecks of the world, against his back. The wind was violent and it wouldn't end. He grabbed the metal rails, his arms straining against his own decision. The blood in his body swirling up in waves. The violence, the pure white heat of it, made him part of some universal electricity. Harry shut his eyes and screamed. Then he regretted screaming. Regretted everything. Not in words. Everything was electric blue, and rancid meat somewhere, and the glossy steel rails he clutched. The train's engine blasted like the entire industrial revolution condensed into a single howl. The sound all encompassing. Harry's mind was metal and steel. Now, he thought. Now!

But no. Here was a different now. The train whistled past on the other set of tracks, not his tracks at all, headed to Philadelphia, then New York. Not Chicago. Not the westbound train at all. Harry sat there on the other tracks to Chicago, Omaha, Denver.

The train rumbling east right beside him was a daisy chain of cars fastened together, a rhythmic conga line that seemed it would never end. He thought he saw the word FORGIVENESS spray-painted on one of the cars.

The train roared beside him chanting: *Not tonight. Not tonight. Not tonight. Not tonight. Not tonight.*

When it finally fully passed, a high singing hum rose from the tracks. Then even that noise evaporated into the late-night sky. Crickets. A dog barking the next block over.

Harry wanted to scream again but he couldn't. He quickly sucked in the night air and exhaled an animal sound he didn't know he was capable of making. He trembled and couldn't stop trembling. And he couldn't let go of the rails at his sides.

After a while he managed to work his left hand free and used it to pull his right arm awkwardly to his side. He wrapped himself into himself, one arm over his head, pulling Harry down.

His head on his knees. Sweat ran down his back even though he had never felt so cold. He wept hard into his still vibrating hands, rubbed his face. He sobbed until his body ached. Then gagging and heaving, he threw up the dinner he'd made hours before.

He swiped his face with fingers that now felt too big. His hands giant mitts, his head a tiny balloon. His flesh pimpled in the shrill night air. The hair on his arms stood straight up. To calm himself he pressed thumb to pointer finger, thumb to pointer finger and rubbed soft circles along his fingerprints. After a time he decided to stand. With great effort he stood as if for the first time. He remained there for what seemed like hours, tottering on his shaky legs.

This is how Harry Kane found himself standing naked in the middle of his hometown, drunk, shivering in the cold. But alive.

"Jesus," Harry said out loud. And then a few seconds later, "Jesus! Why am I such a fuck-up?"

Okay, Harry thought, okay.

Harry walked back toward his tiny home, pushing himself now between the shadows, his stomach cramping, looking to his left and right. He crouched behind a tree as a car turned down an empty side street. Another car passed that looked like his mother's Honda, but that couldn't be right. He clutched his palms into fists, imitated a man who had a reason to walk naked down a street. He passed an empty birdbath suddenly backlit by a garage's automatic safety light. He heard the fluttering of night sounds. A rattled garbage can lid. Scurrying, victorious raccoons. The reluctant glimmer of a last star at the horizon line.

Finally Harry made his way up the dark walkway to his home. He picked up the keys, picked up the newspaper, let himself back in.

The next morning a nauseous sickness descended on Harry. Obvious when his mother called to say hello. Quicker than it seemed possible, she was over with chicken soup, a hint of tarragon, and fresh whole wheat noodles. She let herself in with her own copy of the key she had insisted upon when he signed the lease. The click of her heels across his kitchen floor. Her rosy perfume that would linger long after she left the soup, a box of Kleenex, and copies of a popular antiques magazine she had subscribed to but never read.

Before she stepped out the front door, before she dove into her always-busy day, his mother hovered in the doorway, eyed the neatly stacked pyramid of clothes on the corner of Harry's desk. She walked forward to touch the pile, as if reading the clothes in a language only she and her son spoke. She moved the stack to the chair, turned off Harry's desk lamp, cricking her neck to the left and then the right. She screwed the cap back onto the bottle of whiskey, set it into the empty garbage can beside the desk. She placed a hand to the front of her neck, settled it there for a second. She wanted to say something but didn't know what. Finally she said, "I love you very much, Harry." And then, "I like the new blind." She said it loud enough for him to hear from the bedroom. She did not expect a response, but she stood there a moment anyway before closing the door.

7:23 p.m.

Paint your nails. Inhale. Exhale slowly. Let the paint dry. It's easy. This waiting.

Once the nails are dry, do the dishes. Slowly, deliberately. Dry each plate, each cup, each bowl. Close each cabinet door without letting it make a noise. Inhale.

Vacuum straight lines in the carpet. Dust with the kind of precision your mother would be proud of. Exhale.

Think, think, think.

Check the machine for messages. When the solid red light is still solid and red, put your hands on your hips. Look up. Keep looking. Stand that way until your whole life clings to itself and settles at the base of your spine.

Take a shower. Exhale.

Look at yourself in the mirror. Suck in your stomach. Stick it out as far as it will go. Get dressed.

Imagine the phone will ring the minute you make yourself rush out the door.

Rush out the door.

As you walk to the bus stop, recreate the message word for word. It ends with love and a soft click.

Wait for your bus. Look up the street and down. See hope in the stoplight, the car alarm, the corner deli's lighted sign. Watch the bus come screaming in.

Let it leave the curb without you. Let it pull away.

Squint. Raise your hand to your eyes.

Wait for the next and the next and the next.

Sleep 1969

Perhaps the baby owl was a sign as it came down outside your boyhood window—new feathers tousled, shocked and mourning the loss of easy flight. The short hoots. Over and over. Lost as it was on your rooftop in Omaha, Nebraska, 1969.

Or perhaps it was the boy dreams all around you, the five brothers grunting and gurgling earthy dream noises of the hunt, the kill, the escape. Or perhaps it was the moon, the thunder, the baby owl, the night. And you—there—magically awake to see this disaster of an attempt.

The big man and your mother in their rocky boat of a bed right next to the wall with chinks in the plaster you tried to stop-up with cotton balls lifted from your sisters' dresser the night before. Perhaps it was the creaking springs, or the moment they stopped and the house took an inhale, deep, long, oblivious to the tiny owl—out there on the roof, a jumble of feathers. Streamlined a few moments before, gliding in the crisp, flat air of the Great Plains, now tousled and hooting.

Touching the panes of glass with your thin fingers—wanting to make it real—the owl, hooting. You, there, in a rustle of hand-me-down pajamas, sheets, blankets, thoughts—not knowing this moment would never really end.

And when the mother owl in her magnificence swooped down—after hours, after what seemed like days but were hours, the mother coming to rest beside the baby—maybe that meant hope.

Conduit

At the Wild West bed and breakfast, Alex arranged flowers on the nightstand. On the Vegas Strip, he gave his cab driver a box of chocolates. An electrician by trade, Alex hadn't set foot out of Detroit in many years, but now every two weeks he took a vacation, just like he'd promised.

Alex didn't mind his work. He enjoyed the idea of stringing something nearly alive between walls. He liked sitting in his cold truck drinking early morning coffee from a paper cup.

When Sally came down with breast cancer, Alex didn't know how to stop working. Later, he stood beside her bed, apologizing. They never traveled like they said they would.

As he kept his vigil, Sally disappeared right there before his eyes, hollowing out as each day passed, her breathing echoing his regret with each raspy exhale. One day she could barely speak, her voice like the fall leaves outside their window. Alex leaned in close to hear her. "I want to think about you out there getting lost. You in new clothes and a fancy rental car. After," she said.

Alex knew she would not haunt him. He didn't believe in that sort of thing, and she had always been efficient and practical one. But still, he missed her and hoped she would show just once or twice. He didn't want to let her down if she did. So he made plans, searched the internet, scored deals on hotel rooms, made reservations for planes, trains, fancy cars, and buses. But once he was someplace, settled in his hotel room, he never really knew what to do.

San Francisco, for example, the sun's rays reaching down like fingers through the scattered clouds to the Golden Gate Bridge. My God Sally, get a load of this, he wanted to say. And he cried then. Blubbering in public like a toddler after a tantrum. A big burly guy with calluses on his thumbs in stiff new clothes gripping the rail of the Golden Gate Bridge.

These days friends and family were forever trying to cheer him up, to change the subject. Talking about Sally was off-limits. They seemed surprised at how he couldn't get over it and move on.

When he finally stopped crying and rubbed away his tears, he looked up to see a woman looking at him over bifocals. She wore a cashmere sweater and practical walking shoes. Seagulls circled. Alex followed their arc, looked down to the water, and then back to the woman.

"No," Alex said.

"Excuse me?" the woman said. When Alex said nothing, the woman reached into her purse and handed him a twenty-dollar bill. "Eat something. You'll feel better," she said. Then she strode away.

Alex bought a burrito with the money, a book on fancy cars from a used bookstore, and a smashed penny with the bridge imprinted on one side.

Later, he ate sushi and rode a cable car. The air itself lit up that city, that's what he told people later. "I never once considered jumping," he also said, and not one person thought that was funny. Sally would have snorted milk out her nose. She would've given him her sly secret smile that said only I can love a man like you, only me, no one else.

A few months later, Alex signed up with an Elderhostel tour group, qualifying by just a year. The Grand Canyon, he thought. Can't go wrong there.

The other widowers in the group were both a comfort and a broken record for Alex. Their whining helped him understand how his pining for Sally had the potential to bug the shit out of everyone. Martha talked about poor Richard. And Jenny talked about brave David. Alex himself mentioned Sally once at the beginning, saying she hated organized trips.

They arrived at the Grand Canyon, stood there looking down into the massive gorge. They zipped up their polar fleece and prepared to descend into luscious early morning rock beauty. The cold desert air perked Alex right up. They could see their breath. Like a herd of cows, Sally would've said. Sally would've wandered off to the souvenir shop, refused to member-up for the tour. So Alex did just that. Gave the slip to Jenny and Martha and Rich and Kay in their matching tracksuits.

In the shop he fingered some key chains. He shook a snow globe that sent sparkles over the plastic canyon. Nifty, Alex thought, and paid up. He propped the snow globe on a rock that allowed a good view of the widening expanse. Alex adjusted it a few times to get it right, as if the snow globe was somehow Sally's view of the gorge. Then he wandered back to his people. He smiled at his herd, listened with interest to the history that their energetic leader Sammy let out bit by bit.

They rode mules. They learned about rocks and birds and snakes.

Heading back up, Alex missed having a firm hand to hold, missed Sally's muttered jokes. He tired of traveling in spite of her instead of with her.

Later a thunderstorm rose up over the canyon, clouds forming in a frenetic choreography and letting loose a heavy spatter of rain. Alex hoped he'd see lightning as he leaned back to see the show. Everyone else scampered to the tour bus for cover.

"Thunder!" he yelled, and there was thunder. "Lightning!" he yelled, and he raised his hands above his head and closed his eyes. There he saw the tiny world inside the sparkly snow globe filled with glitter and love. "Lightning!" he yelled again pushing his hands up into the sky as far as he could reach.

Monkey Head

"Rowdies and day-trippers, that's who I'm with," Ryan says cautiously. Seven years old. Where does he get this stuff?

"Where do you get this stuff?" I ask.

He peers over his comic book, a red spider scaling a yellow wall on its cover. "It's just the truth," he says without blinking. "The truth will set you free." He's precocious, everyone agrees. I worry about his future in this unforgiving world.

The minivan smells like breakfast. Ryan's Spider Man T-shirt is already stained, and his nose is running a little. But still, he's cute.

Ryan isn't my kid. My sister's. But I claim him some days when I need a boost, when I need to practice having a normal life. Ryan is always steady in a crazy, unsteady, beat-poet-Hallmark-card kind of way. He slaps the comic closed. "Got to get going, sister."

I'm dropping him off at school. Sometimes I embarrass him, I think, already. He wants to get out of the van fast. "You're swell," he says, all sincerity and dimples, giving me a quick peck on the cheek. Maybe he'll become trouble in high school. But for now he's all innocence and nerdy bravado. I wave, and he ambles good naturedly up the school's walkway with a couple friends.

Stealing Ryan in the morning helps my sister out and gets me out of the house—jump-started. It makes me feel like I have a life with goals and meetings and deadlines. I'm dressed with teeth brushed and I've eaten breakfast, and it isn't even nine a.m. Still, I sit there behind the wheel of my sister's van staring at the super blue morning sky above the school's rooftop until a spirited parent honks that it's time for me to give up the prime drop-off space. Ryan's nowhere in sight. I ease out, decide to stop by Tony's for just a sec on the way home.

Tony is behind the counter at the pawnshop, as always, with his neatly tied ponytail and his cigarettes carefully aligned with his lighter on the glass showcase. He makes me coffee even though I insist he doesn't have to. He carries out this thick, silky black stuff in two bright blue vintage mugs. He knows it's the best cup of coffee in the city, and he refuses to divulge his secret recipe.

It's a typical pawnshop, cluttered with the smells of a hundred different homes. He calls himself a connoisseur of dust. A line of guitars lopes along the ceiling like a gaudy necklace. A few of the same instruments rotate in and out. In fact, I got to know Tony through an ex-boyfriend musician. Pawn the guitar, get clean. Free the guitar, relapse. Stevie, the ex, is a sweet guy, and sometimes I still see his face on poorly copied flyers tacked to phone poles in the South End.

Today Tony's new addition is a fine bowling bag with a ball, shoes, shammy cloth, and a slim, custom pencil that says JANET in soft cursive script down its side. The bag makes me sad, which Tony can see right away so he pulls out a shrunken monkey head. "I can't keep these things in the place. Big run on monkey heads lately," he says, nodding its face toward me.

I immediately think Ryan would love it. I pet it like a puppy. "These are illegal or something, right?" I ask.

"Probably. But we don't think about that here, do we? We just think about wanting, letting go. That's my day." Tony combs his fingers through his goatee. "Day after day."

"How much?"

I buy the monkey head. Tony pats my hand gently after putting the head into a used plastic bag. We're just friends, but sometimes I think he wouldn't mind something more. He deflates whatever moment is building by saying, "I don't care what they say about you, Katey Lynn. You're all right."

Then I'm back in the minivan that I was supposed to have back at my sister's an hour ago. I turn off Ryan's pop station, tune it to the a.m. show that plays honky-tonk and polkas. I take all the shortcuts I know to avoid the lights and am in my sister's driveway in no time flat, the minivan all in one piece, Patsy Cline crooning from the speakers.

Suzy steps onto the front porch in her stocking feet—something our mother forbade for our entire growing up. She steps back inside, returns with her shoes on and her handbag slung over her shoulder.

I kiss her on the lips with a smack. "Gosh, you're swell," I say. "We're happy every day, aren't we?"

"Have you been drinking?" Suzy says. I don't technically have a license anymore, but that topic is not on the table.

"Not yet," I say and hand her the keys. "What is all that extra shit on your key chain anyway?" I hand her the bag with the monkey head in it before she can answer. "Just don't look inside, okay? Just hand the bag to Ryan. He'll know what to do with it."

"Okay," Suzy says.

"Yes," I say.

"Exactly what drugs are you on?" she says.

"Yes," I say.

"I need to get going," she says.

"But you'll give it to him, right? Without looking inside."

"I will," she says, as she fixes the rearview and side mirrors that I didn't touch. "You need a ride somewhere?"

"Me? Nope," I say. Suzy has her hand on the gear shift.

I walk down the street in the opposite direction. I can hear her change the station to NPR news. I hear her shift into reverse, back out of the driveway, throw it into drive, and race away.

Birds cackle, and I watch a squirrel try to bust into a bird feeder. A UPS truck stops ahead of me. The driver grabs a box and strolls down the sidewalk all in one fluid motion, whistling some kind of show tune. He nods my way. I like to think he's checking me out as I continue past him, but I don't look back.

I walk all day. I walk the entire time Ryan is in the brain-washing machine of his little fancy private school. I take a long circuitous route into town, a route that loops by three of my favorite afternoon bars. I happen to keep myself in the vicinity of Ryan's school as late afternoon nears. I can't stop the voice that keeps telling me Suzy won't give him the bag.

Hours pass and finally I'm sitting under a nice shade tree near the parents' valet depot. Suzy pulls up, parks, and comes to sit with me.

She pushes her sunglasses up on top of her head and looks me over. "Sorry," she says.

"About what," I ask.

"About what I said," she says.

"What did you say?"

"Good," she says. "Nothing."

We have a nice conversation. We talk about how our mom fucked us up and agree for once on how and why. "You just wait until you have kids of your own," Suzy says.

"Yeah, right," I say.

A color-coded wave of kids busts out from the school's front door. "Free at last," I say.

"Oh stop," Suzy says. "I'm paying out my ass for this education." She smiles brightly at the other parents. I scowl, grab the sunglasses from her head, and slide them on. They feel luxurious. I wonder if Suzy has whiskey back at her house. Ryan shows up and says, "Those sunglasses are quite becoming, Katey Lynn."

His mother and I look at him. "Stunning even," he says, as he settles into the van's back seat, clicks his seatbelt.

"Okay, you can have them," Suzy says, staring at the Jeep in front of her in line.

"Thanks, Ryan," I say.

"No prob," he says.

As we inch toward the exit, Suzy pulls the bagged monkey head from under her seat. "Here," she says, handing it to me.

"Here, buddy," I say. Handing the bag over my shoulder.

Ryan peeks in, a smile already forming on his lips. "Awesome!" he says. "It's exquisite, Katey Lynn."

When I ask if she has any whiskey at home, Suzy offers to drop me off at Tony's place. She says nice things to me as I'm getting out of the minivan. She doesn't want anything to get started. Or maybe she feels sorry for me. At any rate, happy hour will not continue at the kitchen counter of her ranch-style mid-century modern. Ryan has set the monkey head aside. I'm now sure he was just being polite, or facetious. This starts an itch under my skin. I say, "Thanks for the lift, Suzy. Bye sweetie." I peck Ryan on the cheek. I hand the sunglasses back to Suz.

"Wow, that's amazing," Tony says when I walk into the pawn shop and the little doorbell dings.

"What?" I say.

"Oh nothing. I just knew it was you," he says.

"How? Why?"

"Fate," he says, smiling. "Plus, guess who just pawned his guitar?"

There's no mistaking it. It's Stevie's guitar. Pawned again. "Fuck," I say.

"Yeah," Tony says. "I'll put a hefty price tag on it so it'll be here when he comes back for it."

Seeing the guitar makes me miss things I didn't know were lost. I sit down in the folding chair by the register. "He liked it," I say. "He loved the monkey head. Best present ever."

Tony's looking at me, and I don't have anything else to say. After a minute he says, "Hey, what're you doing tonight? You want to go to dinner and maybe a movie or something?"

I stare him down, wishing I still had those sunglasses. I

slide the bowling bag out from behind the chairs, pull on its wide metal zipper, and dig out Janet's shoes. They're a perfect fit.

"Okay," I say, relieved that for once I might have found the right answer.

Ball and Chain

"**I**'ll be ready when the time comes," my mother says, mocking me.

That's my mom. Holding me to words I uttered at sixteen, or five minutes ago. The sun streams across the café table. She'd have a cigarette lit and smoldering in an ashtray if they still allowed such things.

She repeats, "I'll be ready when the time comes." She means ordering her brunch, she also means dying, death. She's like that. Likes to hear herself talk. Apparently, I said something like this once, regarding death, when I was fifteen or something.

The café chirps bright and happy. Quaint tables with their round-back chairs. Everything intimate and charming here. Mom loves the pecan pancakes, but won't admit it until the waitress comes. I love the goat cheese and spinach frittata. We are consistent with our adorations, always have been. People talk, talk,

talk—leaning into one another—all around us. The espresso machine spits into the milk. Our waitress floats her way over as if she's just wandering by, but then she stops short and smiles. My mother smiles at her. "Lovely day," my mother says. Then, "I'm ready."

I look at her quickly, eyes wide, as if she might drop over dead any moment, and she seems to get the joke. Instead, we order. And we don't talk about the death hovering around us, not here, but out there. Once we get back into my childhood home—we will. Appointments and whispering hushes about my dad, her husband. Everything quiet and gauzy. Words slowed down to the slightest syllables.

For now, we pretend we aren't those people, and play out this happy story here in the café where we used to go after shopping sprees. My dad was never invited. It has always been just us, talking new bathing suits and padded versus unpadded shoulders, talking peg leg, boot cut. We roll with the fashions with the best of them.

Dad seemed proud when we carted home those handled shopping bags. He always smiled like: "This is America, and I'm part of the dream. I work so you can go buy all these things you never wear. This is my destiny, and I'm doing my part." Unlike other dads, he never made fun of our shopping. Never made fun when Mom changed out the holiday tablecloth each year going from harvest leaves to snowmen to Easter eggs. He gathered all the pride in. Now, though, pride is not on his mind. Breathing is his biggest concern.

Mom picks at her food. She says, "Ball and chain. What a strange expression." She only lets me in on half of the conversations in her head. Then she looks at me for input.

"Yes," I say with caution. "Ball and chain is a strange expression." I take a small bite of my toast. Rye. "Butter is so good, isn't it?" I say.

"He said that once," she says.

"Who?"

Mom looks at me then, like I'm not her daughter at all. "He called me his ball and chain," she says. "Dad. Early on. I swore at him, and then left the house for two days. Wouldn't come back." She laughs, a girlish kind of chuckle I've never heard from her before. For a second, I glimpse her, younger, with long red hair, a mischievous smile, freckled, taking pride in her outbursts. It's hard for me to imagine her swearing. She must be exaggerating, two full days? She was squelched long before I came along. Although once I remember my mother spilling furniture polish and saying, "Sh—ugar. Sugar." And I remember repeating that to my father when he spilled his coffee. That morning with the windows steaming up in the cold kitchen. I remember my father giving my mother "the look." And my mother settling into herself just a little bit more, stirring the oatmeal, tapping the wooden spoon crisply on the pan's side.

"You left for two whole days?" I say. "Where did you go?" I sip my coffee as if I'm not nearly as intrigued as I am.

"Oh, I went here and there," she says. A triangle of pancake perches on the end of her fork. "He got the picture though. He understood that he wasn't the only one who made the rules. I think he got it." She chews thoughtfully. "I was ready though, wasn't I?"

Our waitress surfs her way toward us, holding the coffee pot aloft.

"Yes," Mom says. "Yes, I was."

Snowed In

I t's like a silent movie as we make love in the gray morning fog. We're each in our own worlds, living our own parts. We used to talk, to coax each other through our sex. We used to need to murmur, to trace our past as we traced shoulder blades and nipples—we needed to reassure each other that the present was safe, even in the frenzy of our bodies. Now, with the cold seeping through the cheap windows, with mounds of blankets on the bed and the cat pacing and meowing first around the bed frame and then up and down the stairs—later, I'll notice her bowl is empty, that she has tipped over her water bowl again—for now, we are beautiful in black and white. Our lives are easy, our bodies smooth.

Moments end though, like a kettle boiling. The nice moment tweaks and rumbles, and then the whistling brings a whole new day. He's late again. He's shuffling for boxers and hopping around the room to stay warm.

He pecks me on the cheek, "Happy?" "Happy?" "Happy?"

I smile and push him away. I smile and gently grab his earlobe. I smile and push myself out of bed. "Sort of." "Sure." "You bet." I smile and find a T-shirt, a flannel shirt, a sweater. What does happy mean? I find my long underwear, wool socks, jeans. I find my slippers and carry them down to the kitchen, set them on a chair while I make coffee.

Soon I'll sit on them, spill my coffee as I jump up. Soon the phone will ring and it won't be a telemarketer. Soon he'll come down the stairs. Shaven, teeth brushed. Soon he'll go out the door even though all the buses are delayed, even though we've heard cars sliding with tires running blind all morning, even with all the forces against him, including the wind that has started up, he will head out that door, and I don't know why, but I'll know he needs to go. He has forgotten his coffee, and soon he'll call to let me know he's forgotten his coffee, but by that time I will no longer be answering the phone and his message will stay on the machine for weeks.

I've called in sick to work. I've found the novel I started a year ago. I think about making dinner, the kind I used to make. I'm on my second cup when the phone rings. I don't even think, I just pick it up like I'm in the seventh grade and my friend Vera is calling to tell me who did what stupid thing. "Hello," is the stupid word I say into the phone. And a voice—familiar—sighs. Starts to say something. Begins to cry.

There is a time in one's life when a person gets to rise above all the mess of appointments and emails and vacuum cleaner belts snapping—when a person gets to float up, look down, and time stops. A snapshot. A life beginning and ending and starting again and again and again.

And my ears hum. My life hums. I walk from room to room—looking at my things, all of my many things. So when he calls, leaving the message about the forgotten coffee, he is already a thing of the past. The coffee is in the past—our morning, our voices, our life, it is back there in that different time. This time, on the other side, has little room for such details.

Ashes

The yellow wall and a window—the light filtered through is a velvety blue. A lamp shaped like two Siamese cats, shoulder to shoulder, sits on the neighbors' sill. When the lamp is plugged in the cats' eyes light up. Jocelyn knows this, but their eyes always spook her.

Jocelyn walks through the woods in the early morning. The mist and dew settled all around. Squeaky sneakers slush through the tall grasses. The trees soar up—sentries, calm and cool. She stops to pick at a tree's bark and listen to the sleepy birds just getting going with their shrill one-note whistles and tiny *tweet tweet tweets*, and then continues on her way.

Up ahead, she sees red-and-black flannel, someone in jeans walking along. Uncommon this early. Jocelyn has been studying the mosses and has strayed from the trail to climb a large rock with frilly, lacy green lining its top and side. Like carpet. She daydreams about moving into the forest. Building a house that has trees soaring up through it and real moss carpet to dig her toes into. From atop the rock Jocelyn spies the flannel moving slowly, examining this and that. It's another woman, older than Jocelyn. Gray hair pulled back into a ponytail. She carries a little box, like a silver lunchbox, at her side. Wears hiking boots.

Jocelyn wants to call out in a kind of comradery. But what would she say? Instead she studies the woman as she makes her way along the trail that edges the ridge. She wishes she owned a dog that would bark right about now. Jocelyn fingers the cool, soft moss—pushes it this way and that. Then the woman is gone into the darkest part of the woods.

After her morning walk Jocelyn dresses in business attire and heads to an office on the fifth floor of the historic Rayne's building downtown. There, she answers the phone and organizes her boss's life. Sometimes she picks up Mr. Snyder's dry cleaning. She doesn't mind. She's good at keeping everything running smoothly, and they both know it. In fact, employees sometimes buy her snacks and gifts and flowers and pray she will never quit because the company would be lost without her. Today one of them offers her a puppy from their dog's litter, free.

Jocelyn smiles while she works. She types, files, brews coffee, organizes the yearly CPR refresher, and then she heads home to her tiny house on the edge of the woods. She watches as the neighbors across the way turn on their cat lamp. She hums as she makes dinner.

The green tub, a clawfoot antique she pulled from the dump and restored, is her daily luxury. There's a small ivy plant hung above the tub nestled into a bright blue pot and slung into a macramé holder. When she's in the tub, water steaming all around her, candles lit, bath salts dissolved, she feels like she's at the exact center of the universe. Jocelyn tunes her radio to the classical station, keeps it turned low. No one knows where she is. No one.

Jocelyn looks for the woman as she walks the ridge trail, strays off her normal course. It's early again, nearly 5:00 a.m. and steam shoots from her mouth as she leans upward, pressing herself toward the place where there's a view. She can see the town from there, asleep. The office building and her company's floor, a stray light glowing like a pinprick near the corner. Jocelyn waits for the woman from the day before with the gray hair pulled back, but she doesn't appear. In the early-morning fog she starts to believe the woman wasn't real.

Maybe someday Jocelyn will grow her hair long, let it go gray, pull it back in a ponytail. But why the lunchbox? A snack for the hike? Spare socks?

Jocelyn closes her eyes, imagines she's the woman in the red-and-black flannel. The box swings by her side with each long step, the cool metal chilling her when it brushes her skin. The heft of it swings the box naturally forward and back. It's heavy, like a brick. Now Jocelyn imagines the box is filled with the ashes of a dead dog. Her dog, her trusty old lady, who barked at leaves and scampered joyously in front of her as she hiked. Her dog has died and her heart aches. Jocelyn had it cremated and now she carries its ashes in her father's old lunchbox, the one he carried to the mill every day of his working life. The father who wanted to buy her a puppy, but her mother would never let him. She carries the dog's ashes to the ridge. She strays on the trail. She opens it up and scatters the dense gray chunks. A few ashes carry on the breeze like morning birdsong as she senses someone watching her.

Notes

The author is grateful to the following magazines, journals, and anthologies that originally published work from this manuscript, some in slightly different form:

Atticus Review: Ball and Chain; Conduit

Blue Lyra Review: Now

Burrow Press: Pittsburgh Women (reprint)

Corium Magazine: Simple

Drunken Boat: Wyoming

Fiction Southeast: Silence, Pushing

Garden Inside was exhibited as part of the interdisciplinary show, *The Garden Inside*, Melwood Photography Gallery, Pittsburgh Filmmakers, with Sue Abramson and Christina Worsing.

Great Jones Street: How I Left Ned (reprint)

I Call This Flirting (chapbook, Flume Press 2004): And Then (Originally published in *In Posse Review*); Back Porch; Birds in Relation to Other Things (*Quarterly West*); Crickets; Czechoslovakia; Digging (*Pittsburgh City Paper*); Everything Here (*Silverfish Review*); Flight (Now "Susan"); Full Moon (*Quick Fiction*); Gypsy

Caravan in Suburbia (Now "Caravan, Suburbia"); House; Las Vegas Women (*Silverfish Review*); Locusts (*Quarterly West*); What If the Locusts Returned? (*Quarterly West*); Nebraska Men (*Quarterly West*); Oklahoma Men (*Pavement Saw*); Pittsburgh Women; Silent Chickens (*Prairie Schooner*); Sleep 1969; Snowed In; This Is What I Want (*Quarterly West*)

Journal of Compressed Creative Arts: A Crowd (excerpt)

Keyhole: Trees; Home

The Laurel Review: Joshua in Town

New Flash Fiction Review: Secrets

New Sudden Fiction: Short-Short Stories from America and Beyond, edited by Robert Shapard and James Thomas (anthology, W.W. Norton 2007): How I Left Ned

New World Writing: Rise and Settle Again (originally Chest Out)

The New Yinzer: Dirt: Lenny the Suit Man

Nothing Short of 100: Sweetie Pie

Pie & Whiskey: Writers Under the Influence of Butter & Booze (anthology, Sasquatch Books, 2017): Dance

Pretty Owl Poetry: I Have This System for Getting Exactly What I Want Out of People; Transplanting

Quarterly West: What It Would Look Like

Revolution House: The Bottle

SmokeLong Quarterly: Ashes

Thumbnail: Monkey Head

You Have Time for This (anthology, Ooligan Press, 2007): 7:23 p.m.; Nebraska Men

Weave: Alive, Almost

Acknowledgments

So many people helped make these stories and this book a reality. Thanks to everyone—editors, writers, friends, and family—for your support and guidance:

Kelly Abbott, Sue Abramson, Liz Ahl, Christopher Allen, Lauren Becker, Randall Brown, Brian Butko, Guy Capecelatro, Diane Cecily, Ceres Bakery et al, Kim Chinquee, Lawrence Coates, Peter Cole, Jeff Condran, Chauna Craig, John Dalton, Bruce Dalzell, Laura Davis, Elvira Eichlay, Grant Faulkner, Kate Flaherty, John Fleenor, Hattie Fletcher, Don and Shirley Flick, Ben Gwin, Tom Hazuka, Yona Harvey, Aubrey Hirsch, Casey Huff, Lori Jakiela, Alice Julier, Alisha Karabinus, Joy Katz, Kelly's Bar Thursday Night Booth Contingent, Michael Kimball, Chuck Kinder, Nancy Krygowski, Peter Kusnic, Tara Laskowski, Kate Lebo, Dana Levin, Elise Levine, Sam Ligon, Ron Maclean, Bob Marion, Tara Masih, Roger Moody, Bill O'Driscoll, Deborah Poe, David Pohl, Meg Pokrass, Ladette Randolph, Hilda Raz, Lesley Rains, Michelle Ross, Jessica Server, Robert Shapard, Sarah Shotland, James Simon, Sheila Squillante, Sheryl St. Germain, Marly Swick, Phil Terman, James Thomas, Chris Tusa, Christina Worsing, and Sandy Yannone.

I'd also like to thank Virginia Center for the Creative Arts, Atlantic Center for the Arts, and the Ucross Foundation, for the time and space to draft and revise many of these stories.

And also, a shout out to the incredibly supportive Pittsburgh literary scene, which includes Littsburgh, White Whale Bookstore, City Books, City of Aslyum Bookstore, and Classic Lines.

Super duper thanks to my editors at Autumn House Press: Ryan Kaune and Christine Stroud.

Endless gratitude to Christine Stroud for believing in my stories.

As always, my world is made so much better for having Rick Schweikert in it.

Design & Production

Text layout and cover design: Kinsley Stocum
This book is typeset in FF Meta Serif and FF Carina, both designed
& published after the turn of the centry.
This book was printed by Versa Press on 55# Glatfelter Natural.